# SHOOTOUT IN CANYON DIABLO

Canyon Diablo offers Lute Latimore a fresh start . . . provided he can live long enough to enjoy it! The plan is simple — go to work as a deputy for his brother Heck, the town marshal. But Canyon Diablo is a hell town, with a reputation for chewing up lawmen, and Lute becomes a target as soon as he pins on the star. One night, a fusillade of bullets changes everything, and suddenly a new trail beckons Lute — a killing trail . . .

*Books by Steve Hayes*
*in the Linford Western Library:*

GUN FOR REVENGE
VIVA GRINGO!
PACKING IRON
A COFFIN FOR SANTA ROSA
TRAIL OF THE HANGED MAN
LADY COLT
A MAN CALLED LAWLESS
DRIFTER
LATIGO
SHE WORE A BADGE
A MAN CALLED DRIFTER
VENGEANCE TRAIL
THE DEVIL'S ANVIL
IN THE NAME OF JUSTICE

*With David Whitehead:*
COMES A STRANGER
THREE RODE TOGETHER

*With Ben Bridges:*
THREE RIDE AGAIN
SHADOW HORSE
THE OKLAHOMBRES

STEVE HAYES

◆

# SHOOTOUT IN CANYON DIABLO

*Complete and Unabridged*

## LINFORD
*Leicester*

First published in Great Britain in 2015

First Linford Edition
published 2016

A catalogue record for this book is available
from the British Library.

ISBN 978–1–4448–3005–7

Published by
F. A. Thorpe (Publishing)
Anstey, Leicestershire

Set by Words & Graphics Ltd.
Anstey, Leicestershire
Printed and bound in Great Britain by
T. J. International Ltd., Padstow, Cornwall

This book is printed on acid-free paper

To
The early morning gang at
Starbucks, #5807

# Author's Note

For those interested in facts, Canyon
Diablo, Arizona, once considered
the most dangerous town in
America, is now nothing but
a forgotten, crumbling,
windswept ghost town.

# Prologue

I'd just got a letter from my kid brother, Heck. As usual it had been opened and examined by the Assistant Warden, but this time there was nothing in it that petty prison rules insisted had to be censored, so I was able to read every word. It was a newsy letter, full of personal stuff about Heck and his wife, Ellie, and their daughter, Marley, which I won't bore you with, but in it he also mentioned something that surprised the hell out of me: he wanted me, Lute Latimore, to be his deputy when I got out next week.

Since he'd only recently become the marshal at Canyon Diablo, I wasn't sure that making me his deputy was a good idea. Not only might folks accuse him of nepotism, they also might resent having an ex-convict and former outlaw for a lawman. On top of that, it's not my nature to tell other people what to do or how to run their lives. I prefer to mind my own business and go on my way hoping they'll do the same.

But those days, with the sour taste of the Civil War still lingering in everyone's mouth, there were very few jobs available for a Southerner, especially if he was also an ex-con with a reputation like mine. Like bad news, it followed me everywhere. There wasn't a damned thing I could do about it either. Unfair as it might seem, once the newspapers called me the most dangerous outlaw in the Southwest, I was stuck with that label. It didn't matter if I'd served my time and paid my debt to society or not, they made sure the stigma would always be there, hovering over me like an ominous black cloud.

So, figuring I had nothing to lose, I decided that once I got out I'd go and talk to Heck and find out exactly what was expected of me. Also, while I was there, I wanted to see for myself if Canyon Diablo was as dangerous as everyone claimed. Even Heck, who downplays everything, described the squalid sprawling tent town and its so-called dregs of society as being 'hell on earth.' And knowing my brother's passion for telling the truth, I believed him. Judas, even the name of the main street sounded menacing, as if it were forewarning folks about the impending perils facing them. Instead of being called Main Street or Front Street, like in most western towns, it was known as *Hell Street*.

And according to Heck, for damned good reason!

More gunfights, more killings, more robberies and more muggings took place on that short stretch of rock-strewn dirt running between the two rows of false-fronted saloons, gambling houses, brothels and dancehalls than in any other town in the Old West — and that included Deadwood, Dodge City and even Tombstone!

Originally the tents had been pitched alongside the gorge to give temporary shelter to the hundreds of railroad workers tasked with building the Atlantic and Pacific Railroad across New Mexico and Arizona and on to California. And but for a monumental mistake made by the manufacturers of the bridge, temporary is all they ever would have been. If all had gone smoothly, the trackmen would have finished laying that particular section of track, the construction crews would have assembled the bridge across Canyon Diablo — as the deep, steep-sided gorge was called — the surveyors and engineers would have congratulated themselves for being so smart and then the whole kit and caboodle would have moved on, everyone continuing their grueling task of building the railroad all the way to the west coast. Nothing would have been left behind but empty wind-torn tents, the remnants of shacks and saloons, and distant memories of a sordid little eyesore known as Canyon Diablo.

But, as is so often the case, fate had other plans.

Just as the workmen began building the pillars on which the bridge was to be mounted it was discovered that the bridge delivered by the manufacturer was not long enough to span the canyon.

That's right. You heard me correctly. The bridge was too damned short!

The surveyors and engineers couldn't — wouldn't believe it. Immediately all work was halted while they checked and rechecked their measurements. They took their sweet time, wanting to be absolutely sure that they weren't in any way responsible for the costly mistake; as a result, the extended delay resulting in hundreds of frustrated workers idly sitting around doing nothing but playing poker, getting drunk and wearing out the local whores.

It was a recipe for disaster that grew more costly and more dangerous with each passing day. Various reasons for the delay was bandied about, each one more fanciful than the last. But despite all the rumors that spread through the town like smallpox, no one knew the real reason for the delay except the bosses. And the bosses weren't talking!

Then one day the truth somehow leaked out: the delay, now over six months, was not caused by material shortages, as everyone had thought, but by the manufacturer's financial difficulties.

In short, they'd run out of goddamn money and were frantically looking for backers!

Winter turned into spring, spring into summer and summer into fall. During those months the railroad continued paying the workmen their wages rather than lose them to other jobs. It was a tactical rather than generous move, because the railroad barons knew that once work started up again they couldn't afford another delay while new experienced workers were rounded up.

But their seemingly benevolent act backfired on them. Led by two bawdy veteran madams, Clabberfoot Annie and B.S. Mary, a bunch of greedy, opportunistic gamblers, storekeepers, saloon- and brothel-owners descended upon the town. Realizing the crews had nowhere to spend their money or to entertain themselves, they seized the moment and pitched their own tents. They kept them open around the clock, enticing the men with a steady supply of cheap whiskey, gambling, and willing whores.

The money poured in. In fact business was so good some of the owners, like Bullshit Mary, replaced their tents with hastily erected clapboard-and-tar-paper saloons. One man, who owned the Cootchy-Klatch dancehall and fancied himself as the next P.T. Barnum, even hired musicians and built a crude stage for his scantily-clad, garter-legged chorus girls to entertain the rowdy, drunken audience.

But whether the places were borderline fancy or nothing but tattered lamp-lit tents, they all had but one purpose and one purpose only: to offer the workers a good time and in the process fleece them.

Word quickly spread throughout the Southwest that the railroad town was wide open. Like bees drawn to honey, outlaws, gunmen, murderers and border trash poured in, their ever-increasing numbers swelling the burgeoning population until by the end of the first year Canyon Diablo boasted of having more than two thousand residents.

Lawlessness was rampant and growing worse every day. With no lawman to curb the violence the freight carriers, lumber mill and sawmill owners and all the various other merchants, both in Canyon Diablo and nearby Flagstaff, saw their chances of growing rich fading. They quickly called an emergency meeting. Everyone agreed that something had to be done to protect their investment — and done fast. The easiest solution was to hire a veteran lawman. But no veterans were available. So money was raised to hire a former railroad express guard to be the town sheriff. Though Heck never met him, my brother said that everyone who knew the man claimed he was brave and honest and there was great hope for his success.

But it was not to be. He was gunned down exactly five hours and six minutes after being sworn in.

Over the next few months five more sheriffs were killed almost as rapidly. From then on there were no more volunteers. Not for any amount of money. And once word spread that there were no lawmen around, more and more outlaws, renegades and drifters made Canyon Diablo their home. Cautious at first, as the months passed the lawbreakers grew bolder. Gunfights, robberies and muggings took place in broad daylight. Shootings became commonplace. Boot Hill had to be enlarged to make room for all the new graves. Undertakers worked around the clock, their mortuaries so overcrowded with fresh corpses that dead bodies often lay rotting in the streets for days. Many citizens, fearing outbreaks of smallpox or cholera, abandoned their homes and businesses and moved away. Before they could be missed, their places were taken by more criminals and riffraff. The shootings, murders and drunken brawls escalated until the few remaining decent citizens feared for their lives every time they ventured out into the streets.

Finally they complained to Governor Frederick Augustus Tritle, demanding that he bring in soldiers from Fort Bowie and place Canyon Diablo under martial law. But the recently-appointed governor was too busy trying to hush up accusations of corruption in his administration to worry about a few unhappy citizens, and their complaints were ignored.

Someone then had the brilliant idea of notifying the newspapers. At once reporters swooped down on Canyon Diablo. They interviewed the citizens who were brave enough to ignore the death threats from gunmen that were against change, and soon headlines and articles describing the uncontrolled violence filled newspapers across the country.

Overnight, Canyon Diablo became known as 'The most dangerous town in America!'

This lurid description made for good copy but didn't please the railroad lobbyists in Washington, D.C. As one, they confronted President Chester Arthur, who'd assumed the presidency after the assassination of James Garfield, and implored him to intervene. If he didn't, they warned, the continued lawlessness would hinder the building of the railroad which, in turn, would affect the overall economy of the country.

Their message hit home. The president promptly ordered Governor Tritle to contact the U.S. Marshal's Office in Phoenix and instruct them to send a deputy to Canyon Diablo. The governor grudgingly obeyed and since Deputy U.S. Marshal Heck was already in Arizona, policing the Gila bend area, he was assigned the job.

I learned most of this from rumors

which circulated through the prison as if there were no walls. I wasn't happy about the news and knowing Heck's wife like I do, I'm sure Ellie was even less happy. But her protests must have fallen on deaf ears because according to a recently-imprisoned train robber I knew, my brother had indeed become the new marshal at Canyon Diablo.

Once Heck and his family were settled in, he tried to hire a deputy. But all the suitable men were too intimidated by the unruly element to accept the position and for the first three months Heck was alone on the job.

Coincidentally, it was about this time that Warden Cox informed me that I was up for parole. Jaded as I was, I didn't believe him. But for once the conniving sonofabitch was telling the truth. The Board paroled me for good behavior and I quickly wrote Heck about the great news. He replied that the timing was perfect. He desperately needed a deputy and could think of no one he'd rather have than me. Was I interested?

Though I've got no use for the law and under normal circumstances would have turned him down, at the same time I knew that with me at his side Heck stood a better chance of surviving. So feeling obligated, as most elder brothers would, I reluctantly and with more than a few misgivings wrote back agreeing to be sworn in . . .

# 1

This, then, was the situation facing me on that cold, crisp afternoon in the spring of '82, when I got off the local stagecoach that ran between Flagstaff and Canyon Diablo. Weary after the dusty, bone-rattling ride I stood there on Hell Street, rubbing the stiffness from my back and squinting in the high-desert sunlight as I looked around for my brother. Then I heard someone shouting my name and turning, saw Heck hurrying toward me.

Though he'd occasionally visited me in prison over the years, he looked older and more harried than I remembered and I wondered if the Deputy U.S. Marshal's badge pinned on his vest was responsible for that. It wouldn't have surprised me. Heck was no fool but was loyal to a fault. He must have known that trying to bring law and order to

Canyon Diablo was tantamount to committing suicide, yet he accepted the task anyway like the good soldier he was. And though no one believed that he or any lawman would live long enough to tame the town, so far he had fooled them. He'd been marshal for a record three months and eleven days now — a minor miracle in itself — and though shootings and robberies still happened on a daily basis, both were occurring less frequently than before he arrived. This and the fact that he'd survived for so long when others before him hadn't, had made Heck something of a legend.

My brother wouldn't have been pleased if he'd known how others were praising him. He prided himself on being an ordinary man, blessed by good fortune, and was quick to shy away from the limelight. Some folks found his humility misplaced. Not me. It only made me more proud of him. And curious to find out how he'd managed to survive for so long, I squeezed through the crowd of folks greeting the other passengers and joined him.

We pumped hands and hugged, and in that emotional moment the years I'd spent in prison faded into memory. Fate had given me a second chance with which to redeem my self-respect and I was determined to take advantage of it. I forced myself to think only of the future and how I could help Heck bring law and order to Canyon Diablo.

A little later, while we were bending an elbow at the bar in the Last Drink, one of the fourteen makeshift saloons lining Hell Street, Heck spelled out my duties. He was more mature than when I'd last talked to him, and I found it hard to believe that this was the same shy guileless brother who ten years ago had fought back tears as we said goodbye outside Yuma Territorial Prison.

I listened carefully as he talked, knowing this wasn't easy for Heck. As my kid brother he was used to following my lead without question.

Now, here he was, my boss so to speak, giving me orders I had to obey. To his credit, he handled what might have been an awkward situation perfectly. He methodically went over each of my duties, ticking them off one by one as he explained why they were important and why I had to follow them and not turn 'maverick' on him. I promised not to, at the same time trying not to question his list of dos and don'ts, but finally I'd heard enough and stopped him.

'Whoa,' I said. 'Hold up, Little Brother. You sure about this?'

''Bout what?'

'Wanting me to be your deputy?'

'What do you mean?'

'Well, no one knows better than you what a short fuse I got.'

'So?'

'So, if some piss-ant drunk or rowdy hothead keeps prodding me, I'm likely to bend my iron over his head.'

'He'll probably deserve it,' Heck replied. 'That and a damned sight more.'

'Maybe. And I'll be more than happy to oblige him. But how's that going to fit in with your orders to 'use restraint' whenever possible?'

'That'll be up to you, Lute.'

'Me?'

'Sure. Once you pin that badge on you're the law. And knowing you as I do, you don't need me wet-nursing you 'bout what's right or wrong.'

He had that straight.

'The thing is,' Heck continued, 'being a marshal doesn't have to be complicated. I learned that from the great Marshal Ezra Macahan himself. When handled correctly, he said, it's a straightforward almost simple job. And in the short time I've been marshal, I've found that to be true. In fact the simpler you keep it, the easier it is.'

I wasn't convinced and I grunted in a way that could have meant anything.

'What it boils down to, *hermano*, is this: use your discretion. Be as fair as you can. And treat everyone equal.

18

That's the secret. Do that and you'll be surprised how well folks — even the worthless lowlife kind of scum that thrive here — respond.'

'Equal and fair, huh?' I said dubiously.

'Yep. And remember: when in doubt discretion's the way.'

'Does that include when some jug-head drunk jams his .45 in my gut?'

Heck sighed and I knew I'd irked him. 'Look,' he said patiently, 'every situation's different and has to be handled differently. I'd be the last to argue that. But even in the worst situations, discretion not only helps to calm things down, it also gives you that extra second you need in order to make the right decision.'

'And if discretion fails?'

'Then follow your instincts.'

'Meaning, shoot the sonofabitch?'

'If that's the only alternative, yes. But for my sake, should that time ever come, be damned sure you clear leather first. I don't want to be responsible for burying the best brother anyone could ever have.'

'Must be the altitude,' I deadpanned. 'You've become delusional.'

Heck wasn't amused. 'Quit joking around, Lute. Other than my wife and daughter, you're the best thing that ever happened to me.'

He was dead serious and I didn't know what to say.

'So what's the verdict, *hermano*? You with me or not?'

'Need you ask? 'Course I'm with you. All the way.'

'Great! I knew I could rely on you.'

'Don't throw a shoe,' I cautioned. 'I'll be your deputy and I'll always back your play. But what kind of lawman I'll be only the devil knows. I promise you this though, Little Brother: I'll do my damnedest not to let you down.'

'I never thought you wouldn't. And you'll be a great lawman. I'd bet my life on that. Just try to rein in that hair-trigger temper of yours and don't shoot every skunk who gives you trouble. Not that the no-good sonsof-bitches won't deserve it. They will. It's just that, what I'm trying to get these yahoos to understand is that we're not like them. We don't kill for the fun of it. We don't lie and we don't cheat. We can't be bribed or bullied. We don't run scared. We're here and here we're going to stay.'

'Jesus,' I groaned. 'You're making us sound like goddamn choirboys.'

'I don't mean to. But as lawmen, we got to live up to higher standards.'

'Little late for *me* to do that, isn't it?'

'Why?'

'You forgetting what happened in Santa Rosa?'

''Course not. I'm not condoning it either. Killing is almost always wrong. But that's history. Just or unjust, you paid your dues and now it's time to get on with your life.'

'If folks will let me.'

'It may take time, but eventually they will. Especially if the truth ever comes out that the man — '

'Judge.'

' — Judge — you shot was being bribed to turn a blind eye to all the shootings done by Stillman Stadlander's gunmen.'

'Stadtlander's involvement was never proved.'

'Your word's good enough for me. And considering his unsavory reputation, not to mention his ruthless lust for power at any cost, it should've been good enough for any honest judge.'

I couldn't disagree with that.

'Anyway,' Heck went on, 'whether folks forget or not doesn't really matter. You're here now and working for me.'

'For which I've never thanked you.'

'No thanks necessary. I could do you a million favors and that still wouldn't make up for all the years you looked out for me after the fever took our folks.'

'You would've done the same for me.'

'I would've tried, that's for true. But I'm not you, Lute. I don't have your smarts or your strength of character.

And without 'em, I doubt if I could've carried the load.'

'You would've carried it just fine, Little Brother. Your trouble is you never give yourself enough credit. You're too busy giving it all to me. No, no,' I said as he started to interrupt, 'let me finish. I'm smart enough. I won't argue that. But if I was as smart as you think I am, I wouldn't have gunned down a circuit judge, no matter how crooked the sonofabitch was.'

Heck shrugged. 'Maybe so. But, like I said, that's history. You're a lawman now, same as me. And as lawmen we've sworn to follow the law to the last letter. And anyone here who doesn't do the same will end up behind bars — and that includes all the outlaws and gunmen that up until now have considered Canyon Diablo their own private killing ground. Their way of life is over! Finished! That's our message, *hermano*! And by God, these lowlifes better abide by it or suffer the consequences.' He paused to see if I had any questions. When I didn't say anything, he added: 'It's also another reason, Lute, not to shoot the trouble-makers unless we're forced to. I want all these no-name drunken misfits to shake in their boots when they see us coming and they can't do that if they're dead.'

'If they're dead, it won't matter.'

'That's for true. Unfortunately, in Canyon Diablo there's always a dozen more gunnies eager to take their place. Death doesn't frighten them. It happens so frequently 'round here that I swear they've grown accustomed to it — to even expect it.' He paused to emphasize what he'd just said, and then said: 'But what they *don't* expect and *aren't* accustomed to — and hopefully, thanks to us, will one day learn to fear — is having to pay for their crimes. Hell, most of these no-good vermin have gotten away with murder for so long, they think they're immune to punishment. You should see the bastards, Lute . . . swaggering around, boasting about their killings and robberies, acting like they can do whatever the hell they damn well please and not suffer any kind of comeuppance for it. Well, not anymore! Not here! Now when one of these sonsofbitches robs or kills someone, or rapes some helpless woman, we're going to make him pay for it.'

'How? We aren't judge and jury.'

'We don't have to be. The governor's promised to appoint some honest judges, men not afraid to say guilty or overrule a verdict delivered by an intimidated jury. Once they're on the bench criminals will finally get what they deserve — life imprisonment or dancing at the end of a rope. How's that for justice, *hermano*?'

'Sounds too good to be true.'

'It's up to us to make sure it isn't.'

'That's a tall order, Little Brother.'

'But worth it.' He paused, his expression suggesting that he had more to say but wasn't sure if he should say it.

'Go ahead,' I encouraged. 'Spit it out.'

'You may not like it.'

'I'll take my chances.'

'Okay . . . ' He thought a moment, searching for the right words and then said: 'I've never told you this, Lute, but I always wanted to make a difference in folks' lives. I didn't know how to while I was growing up. I was too busy clinging to your coattails. But then you went to prison and suddenly I had no coattails to cling to. It was brutal at first and many times I was close to throwing in the towel. But thanks to Ellie, who's got more backbone than ten of me, I didn't. And with her help, I've gradually realized that your incarceration was the best thing that could've happened to me. It forced me to stand on my own two feet . . . and to make my own decisions.'

'I'm glad prison was good for something,' I grumbled.

Heck chuckled. 'If I didn't know better, *hermano*, I'd think you'd become cynical.'

'Me? What the hell would *I* have to be cynical about?'

Heck didn't bite. 'Anyway,' he continued, 'like I was saying. I had to make my own decisions and the first one I made was to become a lawman.'

'Okay if I ask why?'

'So I could make a difference.'

'Been a lot of good lawmen,' I said skeptically, 'and none of them seem to have made much difference. If anything, crime's gotten worse and folks seem meaner.'

'That's for true, *hermano*. And I don't pretend to be a better lawman than the legends who've gone before me. But I got to try, Lute. I just got to.'

'Fair enough,' I said, not wanting to dampen his enthusiasm. 'If that's your goal, I'm all in.' I extended my hand and Heck, with his irrepressible crinkly grin, shook it firmly.

'By God,' he said, his eyes as blue as any mountain lake, 'wouldn't it be wonderful if we could really make this work?'

'More like a goddamn miracle.'

'Sounds like you don't think it's possible.'

'Everything's possible,' I said, adding: 'Hell, if those lamebrain Earp brothers and Doc Holliday can tame Dodge and Tombstone, we ought to be able to clean up this hellhole!'

# 2

The marshal's office was in a rundown shack squeezed between Dawson's Livery and Bughouse Joe's, a clapboard saloon near the west end of Hell Street. According to Heck the original owner of the shack, a cantankerous old prospector named Zebulon Carthage, had built it not so much to live in but as protection against attacks by marauding Utes and Apaches. As it turned out, however, he didn't need it. Though no one remembers how, eventually Old Zeb made peace with both tribes and then to placate the neighboring Navajos married the chief's oldest daughter.

I had to laugh. 'If you can't beat 'em, join 'em.'

'Exactly,' Heck said. Continuing with his story, he said he couldn't pronounce her Indian name but when translated into White Man's lingo, it was Woman

With Knife. When I asked him what she was like, he made a face and said she had the disposition of a rabid wolverine and a voice that chased away crows. Worse, according to custom she braided her long hair and then coated the braids with a mixture of bear grease and moist buffalo dung that gave off a foul smell that any skunk would have envied. Folks crossed the street when they saw her coming and she was forbidden to enter any of the stores or saloons in town. Even more humiliating, none of the eligible Navajo braves would have anything to do with her. Neither would any of the bucks in other tribes. Though they were constantly stealing women from each other, none of them ever stole her. This was the ultimate insult and rumor had it that her father became so desperate to unload her that he gave Old Zeb his treasured black bearskin coat, ten gray wolf pelts and six stolen cavalry ponies to marry her.

Though it's likely the rumors about her were exaggerated, Heck claimed to have met her several years before she died of Blackwater fever and though her stench kept him from getting too close, he remembered her as being fat and lazy with a face uglier than the bottom of a rusty bucket. He also remembered that she hated Old Zeb so much she made his life hell in order to make sure he stayed away from her. Her methods worked. The only night he ever slept inside the shack was on his wedding night and that turned out to be a disaster because Woman With Knife not only refused to have sex with him, she warned him that if he dared touch her, she'd wait until he fell asleep and then cut off his penis and hang it from her lodge pole.

That was more than enough to squash any desire that Old Zeb might have had to bed her. From then on, he never entered the shack or spoke to Woman With Knife again. This may sound like a hardship, but according to Heck it wasn't since Old Zeb preferred sleeping on the ground anyway, his gnarly old body covered by a tattered Mexican serape that was a gift from his first wife, Josefina, who was killed by a drunken soldier's bullet after only one month of marriage. Old Zeb had loved Josefina more than he imagined he could love any woman and her sudden death turned him into an irascible, wandering prospector who never shaved or bathed or changed clothes, and rarely spoke to anyone save his mule, Sissy. He also pledged to never draw a sober breath for as long as he lived and kept that promise for the next eleven years. Then one Christmas Eve night he drunkenly staggered to the edge of Canyon Diablo, intending to take a piss, but instead lost his footing and fell two hundred and fifty-five feet to his death on the rocks below.

Now, years later, as Heck and I dismounted outside his office and tied up our horses, gunshots came from the Colorado. The makeshift shack-turned-saloon was just up the street and Heck and I sprinted toward it. But before we reached there a well-dressed man with slicked back hair and a pencil mustache staggered out. He took a few painful, unsteady steps, hands clasping his belly, and then collapsed in the street. He didn't move and was dead by the time we hunkered down beside him. Heck rolled the corpse over, revealing fresh bloodstains seeping through the dead man's brocaded red vest.

'Wade Foley,' Heck said, picking up the ace of spades that had slipped out of Foley's coat-sleeve. 'Reckon he's dealt his last card from the bottom of the deck.'

'Card shark?'

'Uh-huh. Claimed he was from New Orleans. But knowing what a liar Foley was he could just as easily been born in a whorehouse or on a paddle-wheeler — ' Heck broke off as three miners busted out of the saloon. The smallest one held an old, still-smoking Navy Colt and his bearded, pock-marked face was knotted with anger.

'Was self-defense, I swear,' he blurted

on recognizing Heck. 'Can ask any-body, marshal. They all seen the sonofabitch go for his belly gun.'

'And what provoked him to do that, Cory?' Heck said quietly but firmly.

'I caught the bastard cheating and called him on it, what else? Ain't that right, fellas?' Cory said to his companions.

They nodded.

'He's telling the truth, marshal,' one of them said. 'We was all sitting at the table while Foley was dealing, and seen the whole thing.'

'Fact is,' Cory added, 'I almost caught the S.O.B. dealing base on the hand before, but, well, I wasn't sure so I let it ride. Then the damn' sidewinder done it again and I figured enough was enough so — '

'All right,' Heck broke in. 'I'll look into it. Meanwhile, you three go on home. You've had more than your share of fun for one day.'

'But it's early — '

'Don't argue,' Heck snapped. 'Just do

like I say. Go home.'

Grumbling amongst themselves, the trio grudgingly headed off up Hell Street. But after a short distance, they turned and staggered into another saloon, a ramshackle false-fronted eyesore called: Name Your Pizen.

'Want me to go boot them out of there?' I asked Heck.

'Uh-uh. No point. They'd only wait until we were gone and then go find another watering hole to get roostered in.'

'What about this fella?' I said, thumbing at the corpse. 'We going to just leave him here for the vultures?'

Heck shook his head. 'Undertaker's on our way to the livery,' he said, wiping the blood from his hands on the dead gambler's white silk shirt. 'I'll tell him to pick the body up later, when he's got a free moment. Meanwhile,' he said, rising, 'let's go saddle up and head on home. Ellie will shoot me if she finds out you're here and I haven't brought you by.'

# 3

Heck, his wife Ellie and their teenage daughter Marley lived in a cabin on the eastern rim of the canyon within sight of the unfinished railroad tracks. Built in the winter of 1827 by James Ohio Pattie, a trapper and mountain man famous for trailblazing a route from New Mexico to California, it was one of the perks included in the marshal's job. Eating free at the local food stands was another. Free beer at any of the saloons was a third. These perks, Heck explained we rode toward the cabin, was the Council's way of compensating the lawmen for only paying them a paltry twenty dollars a month in wages.

'Ellie's done the best she could with the place,' he added as we rode along the rim, the scrubland on the opposite side of the canyon stretching all the way to the distant sun-splashed mountains. 'And whenever I've had free time, I plugged up the leaks around the windows and in the roof so we'd stay dry during the rains. It ain't much, I know, but at least it's livable. Once you get inside, though, you'll see there's still plenty of fixing-up to be done.'

'You're talking to the wrong person,' I said. 'No matter how much your place leaks or how drafty it gets when the wind's howling, it beats being caged up in a nine by five cell. That I promise you.'

We'd reached the cabin. It was built upon a flat stone slab, boulders on both sides sheltering it from the winds that swept up from the canyon floor. It looked solid enough but as we dismounted and tied up our horses I couldn't help feeling it was too close to the edge to suit me.

Heck, who'd been studying me as if trying to figure what made me tick, said soberly: 'Must've been ten kinds of hell cooped up like that, *hermano*. It's a wonder you didn't lose your goddamn mind.'

'There were times when I almost did, Little Brother. That's when I'd dig out one of your letters telling me what you and Ellie were up to and how you were looking forward to seeing me and how little Marley was getting all grown up. I'd read it over and over, all the time reminding myself that there was a whole world outside those walls just waiting for me to enjoy it. That would keep me sane and I'd be all right for another week or two.'

'I'm glad I could help . . . ' Heck paused, frowning as if troubled by his thoughts, then said: 'Look, I never told Marley you were in prison. Didn't see any reason to, especially since you were going to be my deputy, so let's keep it between ourselves, okay?'

I didn't like lying, but Heck seemed convinced it was the right decision, so I said: 'Fine. If that's the way you want it, I won't say a word — ' I broke off as Ellie burst out of the cabin. Tall, slim and graceful, with cropped hair as yellow as summer wheat, just the sight of her raced my blood. As she got close I could see the joy in her sea-green eyes and the affection she had for me expressed on her pretty farm-fresh face. All smiles, she threw her arms around my neck and tried to squeeze the life out of me.

'Oh, Lute, Lute, my goodness, Lute,' she exclaimed, her Louisiana accent less pronounced than I remembered, 'I thought you were never going to get here. I mean I kept looking at the clock and wondering how much longer it'd be before I'd see you and Heck riding along the rim till it's a wonder the hands didn't fall off. Thank heavens for school this morning or I swear I would've torn my hair out hours ago!'

Her enthusiasm was infectious. But I didn't need encouragement. The joy I felt at seeing her after all these years burned through me like a fever. I wanted to lift her off her feet and swing her around and around until she begged for mercy. I wanted to hold her and kiss her and tell her all the things I'd thought about her while pacing the years away in my cell. But I didn't. She didn't belong to me anymore. She was my brother's wife, not mine. So, restraining myself, I hugged her and pecked her fondly on the cheek, the fragrant scent of rose petals behind her ears flooding my senses. Then I stepped back so I could get a better look at her.

'Looks like I got here just in time,' I deadpanned. 'Few more weeks of pining away for me and you'd be so skinny a good Confederate breeze would blow you away.'

Ellie and Heck laughed.

'Listen to him,' Ellie said. 'Hasn't even walked through the door yet and already he's sweet-talking me. You going to stand for that, husband?'

'Suppose I could arrest him,' Heck replied. 'But then what would I do for a deputy?'

'I'll remind you of that,' I said, 'when

you catch me kissing this pretty lady behind the magnolia blossoms.'

Again, they both laughed. But for an instant I saw a glint of longing in Ellie's eyes.

'For heaven's sake don't mention magnolias,' Heck grumbled, 'or next thing you know she'll have me planting 'em all around the place!'

'If I thought magnolias would grow here — ' Ellie began and then stopped as a lovely, willowy young girl as leggy as a newborn colt sauntered out of the cabin. No more than fifteen, she had her mother's large blue-green eyes, the strong clean-cut features of her father, and sun-streaked light brown hair that hung so far down her back she could have sat on it. She was jaw-dropping-pretty and the only thing that stopped her from being a true beauty was her mouth: though full-lipped, there was a pouty petulance to it that suggested she was spoiled and sulked if she didn't get her own way.

''Be damned,' I exclaimed, on seeing

her. 'Why didn't someone tell me there were two beautiful women living here?'

The girl, Marley, smiled and openly fluttered her lashes at me.

'Hello, Uncle Lute,' she said, her voice too sultry for her years. 'How was Montana?'

I must have looked puzzled because Heck said quickly: 'We explained to Marley how you were up there riding herd for the Thompsons. You know: our friends, Duane and Ema?'

'O-Oh, yeah, sure,' I said, catching on. Then to Marley: 'Montana was as close to heaven as a man can get, missy. Open range for as far as you could see, windblown grass up to your hips, cloudless skies bluer than bluebells and mountains polishing the sun — '

'I'll be dirty dog,' broke in Heck. 'When the hell did you become a poet, Lute?'

'I don't know 'bout being a poet,' I said. 'But riding fence and pulling night watch all these years tends to straighten out a fella's brains so that he gets a clearer perspective on life, if you know what I mean?'

Before Heck could answer, Marley said: 'I've read that mosquitoes in Montana are big as horse flies. That true, Uncle Lute?'

'Bigger,' I lied. 'And there's so many of 'em, they blot out the sun.'

'Really?'

'For true,' I said, using Heck's favorite expression. 'In fact, many's the time when a cowboy went missing we found out later that mosquitoes had carried him away.'

Everyone laughed.

'Then there's the weather,' I added. 'Summers so hot you can fry an egg in the palm of your hand, while in winter it gets so icy cold you daresent open your mouth for fear your tongue will freeze.'

Marley giggled. 'Know what, Uncle Lute, I think you're fibbing.'

'Maybe a little,' I admitted. 'But one thing I'm not fibbing about is how kind the Thompsons were. Best bosses I ever rode for. They made up for all the hardships. Treated everyone fair and square and paid an honest wage for an honest day's sweat.'

'Fact is, you'd still be there, wouldn't you,' Ellie added, 'if Heck hadn't mentioned I was with child again?'

My jaw dropped in surprise. But I recovered quickly and managed to get my mouth closed before looking too foolish.

'That's for true,' I agreed, again sounding like Heck. 'But for that, I would've had a mighty hard time pulling up stakes.'

'Will you be staying till momma has the baby?' Marley asked. 'Or are you just here for a visit?'

'He's going to be around for a long time, if I have anything to say about it,' Heck said before I could reply. 'I just hired him as my deputy.'

'Really?' Marley scowled at her parents. 'Why didn't you tell me that before?'

Her father shrugged. 'I wasn't sure

until a little while ago that Lute would accept, sweetheart. If he'd said no, then you would've been disappointed and I didn't want that.'

Marley seemed to accept his logic. 'That's wonderful, Uncle Lute,' she told me. 'Now maybe you can take me riding some time? Daddy's always too busy.'

'Be happy to, missy. From what little I've seen, this place looks like God's country.'

'It is,' Ellie assured, ' — especially at dawn or around sunset. Then the colors flooding the sky simply take your breath away.'

'Know what she misses most,' Marley said, 'wisteria. Isn't that right, momma?'

Ellie nodded, and said wistfully: 'It's their fragrance mostly. In the evenings when all my family used to sit on the porch, it would be so strong it made your senses swim.'

Heck, whose expression hinted that he wasn't thrilled by this trip down memory lane, stood up, saying: 'Look, I hate to be a wet blanket, but I got to make my rounds.'

'I'll come with you,' I said.

'Not a chance, *hermano*. Plenty of time for teamwork starting tomorrow. Right now, I want you to keep the girls company. I'm sure they got a million questions to ask you.'

'I know I have,' Ellie said. Then to me: 'Unsaddle your horse and I'll show you where to put your gear. I'm afraid we don't have room for you with us, but Heck put a mattress in the shed behind the house — '

'Cabin,' corrected Marley. 'Houses have two floors, carpets, running water and indoor toilets.'

'How would you know, young lady?' her father asked.

'Because I've read about them in magazines from back east,' she replied tartly. 'Momma's taught me to read properly,' she added to me. 'Better than daddy in fact.'

She had a snooty attitude that wasn't flattering. I sensed that she felt she was better than anyone else and I had an urge to put her over my knee and whale some of the sass out of her. Then I remembered she wasn't my daughter and that it wasn't my place to teach her manners, so instead I said affably: 'Well, that's fine, Marley. Reading and writing's real important these days, no doubt about that. But in this town at least, I'm sure your pa's happy he can handle a gun as well as read a book.'

'I suppose,' she said. She looked at her father, and though he was much taller than her she somehow managed to make it seem as if she was looking down her nose at him. 'But I can tell you this, Uncle Lute. When I get married and have children of my own, they'll go to a proper school, with proper teachers. I don't want them learning their ABCs from their momma, like I have to. We'll also all live in a proper house, same as the girls I read about in the magazines, like *Young Ladies Book* or *Godey's Lady's Book*.'

'Don't believe everything you read,'

Ellie said sharply. 'Remember, the best-laid plans of mice and men oft go astray.'

'Momma, shame on you,' Marley said crossly. 'If you're going to quote someone, at least get the quote right.'

'Sounded right to me,' Heck put in.

'Well, it's not,' Marley said smugly. 'In his poem 'To a Mouse', Robert Burns said *schemes*, not *plans*.'

'Schemes, plans, either way Burns got it right,' Ellie said. 'Look at me, for instance. I grew up in a mansion full of servants with my own nanny, a private tutor, and parents who loved me to death. Life could not have been more perfect. But thanks to the war it all came crashing down. Why, if your father hadn't rescued me from those thieving Yankee carpetbaggers, God only knows where I'd be now. Sold to the highest bidder, most likely, along with all our slaves.'

'Momma, that was different,' Marley chided. 'The war between the states changed everyone's life. But now the war's over and according to the President and Congress, things are getting back to normal.'

'President — Congress?' Heck echoed. 'By God, I swear we're raising a politician!'

Marley ignored him. 'When I'm old enough to leave this dreadful town,' she said, 'I shall go to a proper city like St. Louis or Washington and find a rich husband with a proper job, and our children will go to a proper school and live in a proper house, like they deserve. My goodness,' she added, sourly eyeing her surroundings, 'if I had friends like those young ladies back east I've read about, I'd be too embarrassed to invite them home for supper!'

Heck rolled his eyes at me. 'On that cheerful note,' he said, 'reckon I'll be on my way. See you all 'round suppertime.' He clapped his hand on my back, adding: 'Mighty good to have you here, *hermano*.'

'Mighty good being here,' I replied.

Heck turned to Ellie. 'Take good care

of him while I'm gone. Oh, and try not to run off with the first 'proper gentleman suitor' who happens to ride by.'

'I'll do my best,' she replied. 'But there are so many to choose from these days, I can't promise anything.' To me she added: 'We'll be inside. Come along,' she told Marley, who hadn't taken her eyes off me. 'You can put out the biscuits you baked and some of that homemade jam while I heat up coffee.'

Marley didn't move. 'I made them especially for you, Uncle Lute,' she said in a syrupy tone. 'The biscuits, I mean.'

I wanted to tell her to stop sugar-coating me. But I knew if I did it would not only alienate her but upset the harmony between Ellie and Heck. So instead I said: 'I can't wait to taste 'em, missy. Hopefully, they'll make up for all the beans and sowbelly I ate while riding fence.'

Not giving her a chance to reply, I draped my arm around my brother's shoulders and walked him to his horse.

Neither of us spoke. Heck tightened the cinch and swung up into the saddle. He looked uncomfortable, even embarrassed, and I figured I knew why.

'Don't judge her too harshly,' he said, proving I was right. 'Marley sounds snobby but she's a good kid at heart. She's just at that awkward stage. You know, between child and adult. Got all these pent-up emotions churning inside her and doesn't know which feeling to throw a rope over. As high-strung as she is, it must be holy hell for her.'

'Must be,' I said, tempted to suggest that a good paddling might help. 'But you were right about one thing. She's sure gotten all grown up since last I saw her.'

'Ain't it the truth?' he admitted. 'But then, *hermano*, ten years has aged us all.' He kicked his horse up and rode away before I could find a suitable answer.

I watched him riding toward the grimy sprawling tent town until he

51

disappeared behind a row of false-fronted buildings. Then I gave a troubled sigh, wondering what the hell I'd let myself in for, and walked back to the cabin.

# 4

Ellie was standing in the doorway, staring off after Heck with deep concern. There was no sign of Marley, so I guessed she was in the cabin.

'I know it's silly,' Ellie said as I joined her. 'But no matter how many times Heck comes back, safe and sound, I always get this horrible feeling when he rides off that it will be the last time I'll see him alive.'

Tears moistened her eyes as she spoke. Hating to see her upset, I put my arm around her and said as reassuringly as I could: 'You don't have to worry 'bout my ugly brother. He's like the proverbial bad penny: always shows up, whether you want him to or not. I know, believe me, from a lifetime of experience.'

Ellie smiled despite herself and knuckled away her tears. 'Sounds like you didn't always want him to.'

I shrugged. 'Brothers! You always love each other, but you sure as hell don't always like each other. I mean, you had kin. You know what it's like. There must've been times when you wished they didn't exist?'

'More often than not, I'm ashamed to say,' Ellie admitted. 'And I know they felt the same way about me, because I overheard two of my cousins talking about it once. One hundred ways to get rid of Eleanor, they called the list. They sounded so spiteful and mean it was days before I could speak to them again.' She paused, saddened by her thoughts, and then said: 'Of course, now I would gladly give my right arm to have them here, with me. You know? Giggling like fools as they concocted one of their grand schemes on how they were going to trap a rich handsome man and make him marry them.' She paused, her voice cracking, and for the second time that day became watery-eyed. 'Forgive me,' she apologized. 'Although it's been years since — well, since the pox took them, I always get weepy whenever I think of them. Silly, eh?'

'Not to me,' I said. 'Knowing I had a brother out there, waiting for me, always got me over the hump when things piled up on me in prison. Without Heck and his letters to keep me going, I reckon I would've cracked up long ago.'

Ellie didn't say anything. But I knew what she was thinking because I was thinking the same thing, and after a little I felt obliged to say: 'And you, of course.'

Ellie blushed and immediately pulled away. 'D-Don't,' she said, her voice choked with emotion. 'Please don't, Lute. You promised.'

'I was locked up then. Promises are always easier to make when you're separated by bars and stone walls and not expecting to be paroled.'

'Nevertheless,' she said, avoiding my

eyes, 'you did promise. And I intend to hold you to it.'

'You needn't worry,' I assured her. 'You're Heck's now, not mine. And I would never do anything to hurt him or you. Ever. You got my word on that.'

Ellie didn't answer. She stood there, her back toward me, staring off at the distant mountains, silent for so long I thought the conversation was over. I untied the reins and started to lead my horse away.

'Wait.'

I stopped and looked across my saddle at Ellie, who still had her back to me.

'I'll show you where you can bed down.'

'You don't have to.'

If she heard me, she didn't show it. Without looking at me, she led the way around the side of the cabin. I followed, Cisco plodding affably along behind me. Normally, his complacency would have worried me. Right after I got out of prison I bought Cisco from a horse-trader who made no attempt to disguise the fact that the sorrel had a mean streak. 'I'd be asking double the price if he didn't,' he confided. 'But for the right man, he's a gift at any price. And no offense, mister, but you got a look about you that tells me you got a mean streak of your own if need be, so I'm figuring, all things being even, you're the right man.'

I didn't deny his observation. You don't spend ten years in prison without learning how to survive in a mean-gutted, hate-filled, often-deadly environment. And I'd not only survived but on most occasions had given back as good as I got; maybe better. But in the process, I'd become as mean, or meaner, than the cons around me. So dealing with an ornery sonofabitch like Cisco, who rarely obeys any order without some sort of rebellious act — like a sly bite or a sudden cow-kick — didn't bother me. In fact it kept me on my toes, which is always a good thing. But now, for the moment at least, my mind was on Ellie and our past, and for once I paid no attention to the sorrel's amiable disposition.

Ahead, a decrepit old shack stood close to both the canyon edge and the cabin. It was an eyesore, made out of old reused planking, some of the boards showing rusty nail holes, others so warped and poorly nailed together that gaps showed between them.

'I'm afraid the place is in dreadful shape,' Ellie said. 'But I haven't nagged Heck to fix it up, like I normally would've, because I keep hoping he'll come to his senses and take us all away from here.'

'Be a marshal somewhere else, you mean?'

'Exactly. Or even get his old job back with the railroad. Oh, I know he feels being a lawman is a step up from being a Gandy Dancer. And maybe it is. But it's also a lot more dangerous. And hopefully, one day soon he'll realize that and quit before he's killed. It's not impossible,' she added, as if trying to convince herself. 'I mean there have been times lately when Heck seemed on the verge of quitting. But now, of course, with you here beside him, all that's changed and ... ' Her voice trailed off and though I couldn't see her face, I could tell she was frustrated.

Not knowing what to say, I kept quiet.

Ellie did the same and for a few moments all I could hear was the faint shriek of a Harris hawk circling overhead.

Then, 'Oh Lute,' she exclaimed, turning to me, 'why the devil did you have to show up here after all these years?'

'Where else was I supposed to go?'

'I don't know. Anywhere but here!'

She sounded so angry with me I spoke without thinking.

'You don't have to worry, Ellie. I'm not staying.'

'Y-You're not?'

I shook my head. 'Be gone by first daylight.'

'But what about Heck? He's needs you.'

'I doubt that.'

'It's true.'

'What're you trying to tell me, Ellie?'

'Nothing, I ... ' She broke off, momentarily flustered, then after a long sigh, said: 'He's changed, Lute. And not for the better.'

'Hell, Ellie — '

'No, no, don't misunderstand. I still love him. Perhaps even more now that he's got faults.'

'We all got faults, Ellie. And Heck, hell, he's always been quick to admit his.'

I could tell Ellie wasn't listening. 'All I'm saying, Lute, is it's been ten years since you've been around your brother, and in that time I've watched him get eaten alive by this and other towns and the trash living in them. That's one of the main reasons why I begged him to take us away from here. But all that did was make him more determined to stick it out and prove me wrong . . . which he has, I suppose, because this is a much safer town to live in than when we first got here. But at what price, Lute? Dear God, at what price?'

'Go on,' I said as she paused. 'Tell me 'bout the price Heck paid.'

'It's fairly chewed him up. All the things I loved about him — his honesty and integrity, his willingness to see good in everyone, from beggar to bank robber — almost all of those wonderful traits are now gone . . . and if not gone, they're buried so deep he's forgotten they're there.'

I couldn't or maybe wouldn't believe my brother had changed that much. 'Ellie,' I started to say, but she cut me off with an irritable wave of her hand.

'Oh, I don't expect you to believe me, Lute. And being his brother, maybe you shouldn't. What's more, I'd give anything to be wrong. But . . . ' She flung up her hands. 'Oh, Lute, what's the point in going on? You can't whip a dead horse. Besides, you're here now and if there is anyone in the world who can help him, it's you.'

'Thanks,' I said wryly. 'Nothing like having a yoke to lug around.'

'Your shoulders are broad enough. They can take it. Just remember, though: Heck is your brother and he needs you much more than you know. He'd never tell you that, or beg you to stay, he's too proud. That's why I'm telling you. So you don't ride out of here, thinking you're doing what's right, only to find out later that you were wrong ... because by then it could be too late.'

'Too late for what?'

'For him to get back to being the Heck that I married ... a gentle, decent, honorable man who took on this job believing he could turn this town around.'

'And now you don't think he can?'

'I honestly don't know. Worse, I'm afraid to wait around to find out.'

I frowned, wondering what the hell she was leaving out. 'Reckon when you put it like that,' I said finally, 'it's hard to say no.'

'Then don't. But whatever you choose to do, Lute, promise me you'll never tell Heck about this conversation. Or that I tried to stop you from going. If you do, he'll hate me forever.'

'Why? You got nothing to do with it.'

'Haven't I?'

'No. Not a damned thing.'

'Can you look me in the eye and say that?'

I looked directly at her, deep into her sea-green eyes, but then after a second had to look away.

'I thought so.'

'Dammit, Ellie . . . ' I began but couldn't finish.

Ellie studied me, her expression showing mixed feelings. Knowing her so well, I could tell she was happily relieved in one way, but sad and hurt in another.

'It's what you want, isn't it?' I said.

Her rage was sudden. She balled her fists and I tensed, expecting to be hit.

Instead she blurted: 'Oh, Lute! You can be such a heartless bastard at times.'

'And you can be more confusing to read than smoke signals in the wind.'

Her anger left as fast as it had come and she smiled ruefully.

'What?' I said. 'Why the smile?'

'I was just thinking . . . '

''Bout what?'

'How that's an improvement over your last description of me.'

'Which was?' I said, not remembering.

'That I was 'more dangerous than stealing scalps from a Sioux burial ground'.'

'I was angrier back then.'

'Angry? What the hell did you have to be angry about — then or now?'

'That's right,' I said. 'I'm the fella who isn't supposed to have feelings or give a hoot when I lose my best girl.'

My sarcasm only made her angrier. She gave me a look that should have shriveled me. 'That's so damn' typical of you, Lute. You rode into my life like a lonely twister, stayed long enough to not only batter down all my resistance but ruin me for every man to follow, and then without warning blew away leaving me to pick up the scattered pieces of my heart. Angry be damned! I'm the one who should be angry. Why, I'd not only be in my right to shoot you for what you did to me, but there probably isn't a judge in the whole territory — the whole *country* that wouldn't give me a sympathetic pat on the back as he was pardoning me.'

'You all through?' I asked when she'd finished.

'Not even close,' she said. 'But go ahead. I can't wait to hear your version of Cinderella and Prince Charming. Well?' she added when I didn't answer.

My jaw ached and I realized it was because I'd been gritting my teeth.

'I'm still waiting, Lute.'

'For what? You've said it all. And even if I did have a different opinion, it wouldn't change anything. Not for you or me. As I said earlier, your Heck's now, not mine. And as far as I'm concerned our relationship — the way we once felt about each other — couldn't be more over if it was buried under an avalanche.'

She looked at me, eyes as blue as the sky above with a hint of an angry sea in them.

'Oh, God help me,' she said suddenly. 'Why couldn't they have hung you instead of sending you to prison?'

'Thanks.'

I expected another scathing remark. Instead, she threw her arms around my neck and kissed me, hard and full on the lips.

I was so shocked I didn't respond immediately. Then, wrong as I knew it was, I kissed her back. I kissed her with all the passion I'd kept buried deep inside me for more than ten years, and for a long moment all the promises I'd made myself in prison melted away — leaving me with only the pent-up lust I'd always felt for her.

Then she tore herself away and disappeared around the side of the cabin, the slamming of the front door the only way I had of knowing where she'd gone.

# 5

I stood there, two steps from the rim of the canyon, despising myself so much at that moment I was tempted to jump off the edge. It was a drastic reaction, I know, but it seemed like the only way of ending the shame I felt for dishonoring my brother.

'Uncle Lute?'

Startled, I turned and saw Marley standing before me.

'Momma says I'm to help get you settled in.'

'Thanks, missy. That's kind of her, but I reckon I can handle it.'

'That's what she said you'd say.'

'Did she now?'

'Yes.' Marley coyly fluttered her eyelashes at me. 'She also said I wasn't to take no for an answer.'

'Okay,' I said. 'Since neither of us has a choice, lead the way.' She obeyed me and I followed her into the shack. It wasn't much bigger than a holding chute at the Cheyenne rodeo. Rain through the leaky roof had warped the floorboards and the bang-banging of the wind-blown loose boards was almost as loud as the pounding in my head caused by Ellie's kiss.

I looked around. The small room had been swept clean and there was a folded blanket on an old mattress in one corner. An unlit candle and matches lay atop the blanket while a washbowl and an earthen pitcher of water sat on an old table with broken legs that were tied together with leather strips. They didn't look too steady and I pictured one night a strong wind toppling the table, the pitcher of water spilling over me while I was sleeping.

'If they'd told me you were going to stay with us,' Marley said, lowering her chin and looking up at me in a way that made her eyes seem bigger and more inviting, 'I would have made daddy fix everything up. But of course, they didn't. They don't tell me *anything*. As far as they're concerned, I'm still a helpless child to be seen but not heard.'

'Don't worry about me,' I said, thinking that no one looked less like a helpless child than she did. 'I've slept in a hell of a lot worse places than this, believe me.'

'In Mexico, you mean?'

'Mexico, Texas, Arizona, Montana — you name it, I've slept there. Under all kinds of conditions too. In soft hotel beds when I was flush and on muddy ground or floors full of splinters when I wasn't. If there's one thing I've learned during my years of kicking around, missy, it's that poverty plays no favorites.'

'Why should it?' she said indifferently. 'We're all just passengers on the train.'

It would have been a profound statement from anyone; from a fifteen-year-old girl it was wisdom so far beyond her years I knew she must be quoting someone.

'Who told you that?'

'Momma. Said Grampa Chase used to say it all the time. Said it meant that life is full of peaks and valleys and there's nothing you can do about it, so quit grumbling, enjoy the ride, and continue doing whatever it is you're doing as best you can.'

'Sounds like something Grampa Chase would say,' I said.

'You met him, didn't you?'

'Long, long time ago, yes.'

'Was that before daddy started courting momma?'

Not knowing how much she knew about my past with Ellie, I nodded.

Marley studied me, as if trying to read my mind, then said: 'Why didn't you marry momma?'

I shrugged, trying to think of the most diplomatic way to answer her question.

'It's okay,' she said. 'Momma told me that you two were once good friends. That you thought you even loved each other. That's why I wondered why you never got married.'

'The simple truth is,' I lied, 'once she met my brother, I was never in the running.'

Marley mulled over my words, as if they were gold, and then said fawningly: 'I so envy you, Uncle Lute.'

'Me? Why?'

'You've done so much, seen so many different fascinating places. My goodness, it's no wonder you seem so worldly compared to daddy.'

'I wouldn't jump to conclusions,' I warned.

'I'm not, Uncle Lute. Daddy himself says the same thing whenever he talks about you — which is all the time. And unless he's making it up, and I know he isn't, he's led an almost protected life compared to all the exciting things you've done.'

'Oh, sure,' I said, eager to squash any misunderstanding she might have about Heck or me, 'my life's been exciting all right. I mean, what could be more exciting than swabbing floors and spending

your days staring out between iron bars — '
I broke off, catching myself before I
mentioned prison, and in an effort to
explain away her puzzled expression, added:
'That's right: Iron bars, missy. Thanks
to too much whisky and letting off steam,
I've spent more weekends in jail than
you've had birthdays.'

'You were arrested for being drunk,
you mean?'

'Horse-kissing, skunked-out-of-my-mind-
drunk, yes.'

'B-But I don't understand. I mean,
how could you ride herd, Uncle Lute,
or mend fences for that nice man and
woman you worked for in Montana if
you were — ?'

'Inebriated?' I interrupted. 'I got
news for you, missy, you can't.'

'Then — ?'

'Can you keep a secret?'

She nodded, wide-eyed with curios-
ity.

'The real reason I'm not still working
for the Thompsons is 'cause they fired
me.'

Her petulant full-lipped mouth dropped open but she didn't say anything.

'I know your pa told you it was because he needed a deputy — '

'Daddy didn't *tell* me anything,' she said crossly. 'He never does. Neither does momma. I thought I made that clear. They both treat me like I'm this innocent little angel who has to be protected from everything.'

'Well, now you know the truth.'

I expected her to be disappointed in me, maybe even ashamed that her uncle was such a roustabout. Instead she smiled slightly and said: 'Thank you, Uncle Lute.'

'For what?'

'Trusting me and treating me like an adult.'

For an instant I felt a twinge of guilt. Then it vanished and I said: 'Just remember, not a word to anyone, okay? Not to your ma, your pa or anybody else you know well enough to talk to. Your dad's put his trust in me and I don't want to let him down. On top of that, you can see how bad it would look for him if folks knew his new deputy had been fired for drinking by folks as nice as the Thompsons.'

'I understand,' Marley said. 'And you don't have to worry about me, Uncle Lute. I'd kill myself before I'd tell anyone your secret or hurt you in any way.'

Her loyalty surprised me and at the same time made me uneasy. I had no proof that she couldn't be trusted; yet there was something about the way she looked at me, chin down while she studied me with those alluring upturned amber eyes, all the while smiling that faintly mocking smile, that convinced me I couldn't trust her.

'Well, if there's anything you need,' she continued, as if she'd summed me up and found me lacking, 'just let me know. I feel like we're best friends now, Uncle Lute. And like daddy's always saying, best friends have to look out for each other. And I intend to look out for you, no matter what, because I love you so much.' Standing on tiptoe, she kissed me lightly on the mouth, her lips lingering there for a tantalizing moment. Then she ran out before I could say anything.

Through the loose boards I saw her hurry around the corner of the cabin. I could still taste her on my lips and I quickly wiped my mouth with my sleeve. I know I sound *loco* — that Marley's just a young'un who happens to be my niece — but I felt an uneasy chill run up my back, the same kind of chill you get when someone dangerous is dogging your trail. Then, as quickly as it came, it vanished. Chiding myself for thinking such a dumb thought, I went out to collect my bedroll and saddlebags.

# 6

That night Ellie charred some juicy steaks with a mess of fried onions, greens and mashed potatoes and Marley baked a berry pie that was so good I had to have two pieces. After that we washed everything down with pecan-flavored coffee sweetened with honey. I'll tell you, by the time we were finished eating I was so stuffed I could barely move.

'Now don't expect a meal like this every night, Lute,' Ellie warned. 'This being a special occasion, I figured you deserved a treat.'

''Special occasion?' I repeated.

'Your birthday, silly,' exclaimed Marley.

'Hush, child,' Ellie chided. 'Don't be calling your uncle silly.'

'Oh, he knows I don't mean it that way, don't you, Uncle Lute?'

'Sure,' I said.

'Truthfully,' Marley added, 'did you really forget that your birthday was the day before yesterday?'

'Yep.'

'Serious?'

'Serious.'

'It's just senility creeping up on you,' Heck joked. 'Nothing to be alarmed about.'

'Who's alarmed?' I said. 'Hell, I'm looking forward to old age. Once I'm senile, I plan on doing nothing more energetic than spending the rest of my days rocking myself to sleep on the front porch . . . '

Everyone laughed but Marley. She was too busy trying to get her mother's attention to even hear me. 'Well?' she demanded. 'Aren't you going to give it to him, momma?'

'Give me what?' I asked.

Ellie answered me by rising and going to an old oaken chest-of-drawers in the corner. A once-magnificent family heirloom, its corners were now chipped and the varnish was badly scratched and flaking — souvenirs of its train ride from Ellie's home in Louisiana.

'Close your eyes,' she told me as she opened the top drawer.

'Why?'

''Cause it's a surprise,' Marley scolded.

Heck shot me a look that warned me not to argue. I obeyed.

I heard Ellie return beside me and place something on the table.

'All right, you can open them now,' Marley said, giggling.

Again, I obeyed. There, before me, sat a box wrapped in fancy blue paper.

'I want you to know, *hermano*,' Heck said, 'that Ellie sent all the way to San Antonio for that. So you'd better appreciate it.'

'Don't listen to him,' Ellie chimed in. 'As usual, he's exaggerating. I ordered it from a catalogue and *they* had the *store* send it to me from San Antonio.'

'Either way,' Heck said, irked at being contradicted, 'it's from San Antonio.'

'Well, open it, Uncle Lute,' Marley exclaimed. 'I'm dying to see if it fits.'

'Hush, child,' scolded her mother. 'You want to spoil the surprise?'

I ripped off the paper revealing a thin flat box about a foot long.

'Wonderful,' I joked. 'Just what I needed: a new pair of boots.'

'I wanted to get you a hat,' put in Heck. 'You know, one of those *Boss of the Plains* Stetsons made in Philadelphia. But since I didn't know your size and couldn't ask you without giving away the surprise, Ellie settled for this.'

I removed the lid of the box. 'Damn my spurs,' I said as I unfolded the tissue paper. 'This has got to be the best-looking belt I ever did see!'

'Do you really like it, Lute?' Ellie said anxiously. 'I mean, was Heck right? Would you have preferred a new Stetson?'

'Not in ten lifetimes,' I said. I held up the cowhide belt with its shiny, initialed brass buckle and whistled softly. 'Hell's fire, this makes turning forty-three almost a pleasure!' Rising, I kissed Ellie on the top of her head. 'Reckon I can't thank you enough!'

She smiled, eyes brimming with happiness, and I had the damnedest time preventing myself from wrapping my arms around her and hugging her like I'd imagined hugging her a thousand times while lying on my cot in that cramped, dark cell.

'I'm so glad you like it,' she said. 'After all those years in prison, I wasn't really sure what to get you — ' She broke off with a horrified gasp as she realized what she'd done.

'Prison?' Marley said. She frowned, confused, and looked at her mother. 'Uncle Lute was never in prison. Were you, Uncle Lute?'

'Your ma meant to say jail,' I said, trying to repair the damage. 'Right, Ellie?'

'Y-Yes, of course. I don't know why I said prison, I — '

'See what happens when you drink too much?' Heck teased.

Both were lousy liars and Marley saw through them instantly.

'You're lying, all of you!' she exclaimed angrily.

'Calm down,' began her father.

But Marley was too hurt and furious to listen. Glaring at me, she shouted: 'How could you, Uncle Lute? How *could* you? I thought we were friends!'

'I'm sorry,' I said lamely. 'You're right. There's no excuse. Friends or not, I shouldn't have lied to you. Not for any reason. It's just I wasn't sure how to — '

'Admit you're an ex-convict?'

'Yeah. I reckon that's what it boils down to.'

'I wouldn't have cared,' she said. 'It wouldn't have mattered to me what you'd done!'

'I realize that now, Marley. But — '

'Were you *ever* going to tell me?'

'Sure. When I found the right moment — '

'Liar!' she screamed. 'Liar! Liar!'

'Now wait a minute,' admonished her father.

Marley ignored him. 'I thought you were different,' she raged at me. 'But you're not. You're just like every other grownup! When you're caught lying, you make up excuses — something to blame it on. It's either not the right moment or we're not smart enough to understand or — or too young to know the truth!'

'I've never said you weren't smart,' I said. 'Or too young.'

'Maybe not to my face. But you've said it. So have my folks. I've heard 'em talking. 'Oh, let's wait until Marley grows up, or until she gets a little older and knows what we're talking about, and then we'll tell her.' Adults! You're pathetic, all of you!'

'Marley, stop it!' her mother said angrily. 'Stop it right this instant! I won't have you being rude to Uncle Lute or — '

'I hate you!' Marley screamed at me. 'Hate you! Hate you! And I'll never speak to you again!' She ran, sobbing, out of the cabin.

'It's all right,' Heck said, rising as I went to get up. 'You two stay here. I'll get her.' Grabbing his hat from the peg by the door, he hurried out into the night.

'Damn,' I said, angry at myself. 'Why the hell didn't I just tell her the truth in the first place? It would've solved everything.'

'It's not your fault,' Ellie said. 'It's mine. Good Lord, what on earth was I thinking about letting it slip out like that?'

We both sat there, feeling miserable, waiting for Heck to return with Marley.

Finally Ellie broke the silence. 'Look,' she said, 'while we have a moment alone, there's something I've got to tell you.'

'What?'

'When we were talking before — earlier, I mean — you know, out by the shed?'

I nodded.

'I didn't mean what I said. I don't want you to leave, Lute.'

'But — '

'No, no, I'm serious. I've gone over it a million times and you're right. I *am* Heck's now and what's past is past. Which means there's absolutely no reason for you to leave.'

'I can think of one mighty important one.'

'I don't want to hear it,' she said firmly. 'Now or ever. Do you understand?'

'Ellie, hiding my feelings ain't going to change anything. Or make them go away. I still love you and I got a hunch you still love me — '

'No! No, I don't. What's more, you're to forget you ever loved me. Or that I loved you. All that's behind us now. I'm married. I have a wonderful husband and a daughter pushing womanhood, both of whom I love with all my heart, and that's all there is to it. What we had is over. Over and done with. Do you hear me, Lute? *Do you?*'

'Loud and clear,' I said, adding: 'But hearing's not my problem. I just don't believe you. I haven't stopped loving you and I don't think you've stopped loving me. And because of that, being around you and not being able to hold you or kiss you is driving me — ' I stopped as the door opened and Heck entered, dragging Marley behind him.

Like her father, she was out of breath from running. Her hair was a mess, both knees were scraped from falling down, and she was still furious. She stopped in the center of the room, refusing to look at me. But even with her head down, I saw that her eyes and cheeks were red and puffy from crying.

Heck closed the door and stood beside the three of us, tight-lipped and grim.

'I've told Marley that this was entirely my fault,' he said, addressing all of us. 'I explained that you, Lute, wanted to tell her the truth right from the start, and that it was me — not you, or you, Ellie, who insisted you didn't. I know now I was wrong. For that, I've apologized to Marley. She's accepted my apology and we've both agreed never to mention it again. Or hold any grudges. Isn't that right?' he said to Marley.

She nodded sullenly, but still kept her head down, refusing to look at anyone.

'I didn't tell her why you were in prison,' Heck continued, 'since I figured it wasn't any of my business. If one day you two ever feel like it, you can sit down and discuss it. Maybe clear the air. But that's up to you.' He paused and sighed heavily before saying: 'I reckon that's about it. So if it's all right with you two, Marley's going to bed now. It's her bedtime anyway, so — '

He stopped as Marley, too angry to listen anymore, hurried off to her bedroom.

'Don't worry,' Heck said, reading my expression. 'She just needs time to get over this. Her emotions are all knotted up. You know how easily young'uns get hurt, especially when they care about someone. And Marley cares a ton about you, Lute, and now, thanks to me, feels like you've betrayed her trust. But she'll feel better tomorrow.'

'I wouldn't count on it,' Ellie said. 'I've seen her angry before, but never like this.'

'Maybe so,' Heck agreed. 'But believe me, after a good's night sleep she'll be fine. I'm sure of it. Meanwhile, I'm heading into town to make my final rounds. The Guthrie brothers rode into town earlier. I locked up them for a week a few years back for causing a ruckus, and I want to make sure they aren't planning to stir up trouble again.'

'I'll go with you,' I said, adding before he could argue: 'I need to stretch my legs 'fore hitting the hay anyway and this'll be a good time to do it. It will also give me a chance to get acquainted with the town, and at the same time let everyone know that they've now got two of us to contend with. Make sense?'

'I reckon.' Heck took his double-barreled shotgun off the pegs above the door and turned to Ellie. 'We shouldn't be long, honey. But if you don't feel like waiting up for me, I'll understand.'

'I'll wait up,' Ellie assured him. 'What with all the excitement tonight, and this being Lute's birthday supper — well, I'm too keyed up to sleep anyway.' She hugged him and kissed him fondly on the cheek. 'See you soon.'

'See you soon,' he replied as if the phrase was a ritual between them.

Putting on my hat and heavy sheepskin coat, I buckled on my gun-belt, grabbed my rifle, nodded goodnight to Ellie and followed Heck out the door.

Outside, the windless night air was stone cold. I shivered and buttoned up my coat. I then fell in step beside my brother and together we walked toward Hell Street.

There were no streetlights, making the darkness seem all the more menacing. Off in the distance I could hear shouting followed by shooting.

'Don't let gunfire throw you,' Heck said as I instinctively reached for my

Colt. 'Here that's normal. I'd be more worried if it was all quiet. That'd mean somebody somewhere was probably cooking up trouble, maybe even setting a trap for us.'

'Thanks for the warning, *amigo*. Nothing like being shot at your first day on the job.'

Heck chuckled and we walked on, heads swiveling as we checked out every shack and dark alley we passed.

'You know,' I said as Heck lit a hand-rolled and spat out a stream of smoke, 'I been thinking. Maybe the two of us working together isn't such a good idea. With Ellie expecting, the last thing I want to do is drive a wedge 'tween you and Marley.'

Heck stopped, so abruptly I walked on for a few steps before stopping and returning beside him.

'Let's get one thing straight, *hermano*,' he said firmly. 'If you don't want to be my deputy or feel like moving on, I won't stand in your way or even try to change your mind. But don't use Ellie or Marley, or any other reason as an excuse. Just do what you always told me to do: come right out with it. Shoot from the hip. There'll be no hard feelings. We'll just shake hands and tomorrow I'll be the first to wish you well and send you on your way. Fair enough?'

'More than fair,' I said.

'So what's it going to be?'

'I'll stay on one condition.'

'Name it.'

'Tomorrow we fix up that pigpen I'm going to be living in for the next few months.'

'Or longer?'

'Or longer.'

'Deal.' He rested the shotgun on his shoulder, took a long drag on his cigarette and flipped it off into the night. Together, we continued on toward town.

# 7

On reaching the next corner we swung left and started along Hell Street. We were now at the west end, across from Dawson's Livery Stable, and as we continued on toward the double row of noisy, brightly-lit saloons I noticed Heck had slowed down and seemed unusually tense as he cautiously looked around. I also noticed how white his knuckles were as he gripped the double-barreled shotgun, now held in front of him, fingers on both triggers as if he were expecting trouble.

'What's wrong?' I asked quietly. 'You see something I missed?'

He wagged the shotgun at a tin-and-plank-walled saloon that occupied the next corner on our right. Larger than some of the other shacks, the word Texas was painted in white above the door. The building had no windows, preventing us from seeing inside. But from all the coarse laughter and cursing going on, it was obvious the place was full of rowdy drunks.

'If the Guthrie boys are still in town,' Heck said, 'that's where they'll be.'

I stopped. 'Say you're right. How do you want to handle this? You and me, separate, front and back, or both of us together, busting in the front door, guns blazing?'

About to reply, Heck hesitated and scowled as if angry at himself. 'God-dammit!'

'What's wrong?'

'I almost asked you what you'd do.'

I shrugged. 'Old habits, Little Brother . . . tough to break.'

'Reckon so . . . ' Heck broke open the shotgun, made sure it was loaded then snapped it shut. 'Both of us. Front door. Guns cocked. But no firing till someone prods us into it.'

'Discretion's the way. I get it.' I drew my Colt and held it down by my side as we approached the saloon.

There was no boardwalk fronting it; just ankle-deep dirt, mixed with still-steaming horse dung that clung to our boots as we walked. The pungent stench flooded my senses.

When we were a step away from the swing-doors, Heck said grimly: 'Once we're inside, *hermano*, keep your temper and follow my lead.'

I nodded, at the same time thinking that four eyes were better than two and if I saw something he missed, like some gunny slyly reaching for his iron, I was going to shoot the sonofabitch and apologize later.

We pushed in through the doors. Heck, who was just ahead of me, stopped after a few steps. I did the same, six-shooter still down by my side, watching as my brother scanned the smoke-filled room for the Guthrie brothers.

Everything went eerily quiet. All conversation stopped. The piano player froze, hands above the ivories, while the men crowding the bar all turned and stared warily at us.

'Nobody move!' Heck shouted. To me he added: 'Shoot the first S.O.B. who even looks like he's going for his gun.'

'Count on it,' I said.

Heck spoke to the older of the two balding, mustachioed bartenders. 'I'm looking for the Guthrie brothers, Jake — they been in tonight?'

'Earlier,' the bartender replied.

'How earlier?'

The bartender shrugged fatly. 'Hour ago, maybe less.'

'Say where they were going?'

'Why would they tell me, marshal? We ain't kissing cousins.'

Heck let that pass. Widening his gaze to include everyone, he said: 'If any of you turd-stompers know where the Guthries are, speaking up now will go a long way toward how long you stay in the jug next time I arrest you.'

Silence.

No one moved. No one even blinked. I figured they were too scared of reprisals.

Then a tall, young, bleary-eyed cowboy at the bar drained his beer and wiped his mouth on his sleeve. 'Did I hear you say the next round's on you, marshal?'

Heck nodded at the older bartender. 'Put it on my tab, Jake.'

The bartender refilled the cowboy's glass.

'Well?' Heck asked him.

The tall young cowboy gulped down half of his beer before saying: 'I heard 'em talking just 'fore they left, marshal.'

''Bout what?'

'Some unfinished business they needed to 'tend to.'

'Here?'

'Yep.'

'What sort of unfinished business — they say?'

The tall young cowboy shook his head. He then pulled a bottle of tequila from his jacket pocket and took a swig before adding: 'But they did say that after they got done tending to business, they was headed for Albuquerque.'

'Albuquerque — you're sure 'bout that?'

'Yep.'

Heck mulled things over before telling me: 'We're done here, deputy.'

I slowly backed up, ready to shoot anyone who went for his iron. Beside me, Heck did the same. Our backs bumped open the swing-doors. We continued to back up until we were outside and in the street, the bitterly cold night air making my skin prickle.

'Just my opinion,' I said, 'but could be that tall drink of water was lying, and the Guthries are headed for your place.'

'You're reading my mind, *hermano*.'

'So?'

'Get back to the cabin as fast as possible and make sure the girls are okay.'

'What about you?'

'Soon as I finish my rounds, I'll join you.'

I had a sinking feeling. 'You figure that's wise? Could be that cowboy's setting you up for an ambush.'

'I know,' Heck admitted. 'But I can't let that stop me from doing my job.'

'Caution's the way, Little Brother.'

'Caution — discretion — both good words to hang your hat on.'

'Then why ignore them?'

'Because it's too late to do anything else. I know this town, Lute. Know these people. The word's already on the street that I'm looking for the Guthrie brothers. If I don't run them to earth, everyone will figure I got scared and from then on I'll be the town clown, and may as well turn in my badge.'

'Would that be so bad?'

Heck grunted. 'Been talking to Ellie, have you?'

'Can't blame her for wanting you to stay alive.'

'It goes deeper than that, *hermano*. She wants me to quit being a lawman altogether. Wants me to take her and Marley some place where it's safe. I keep telling her that there is no such place. You can't hide from the bullet that's got your name on it.'

Knowing he was right, I kept quiet.

'Hell,' he continued, 'it doesn't even have to be a bullet. You can work in a bank or a grocery store and think you're safe when suddenly you trip over your own feet and fall, hit your head on something and end up dying just the same as if you'd been shot.'

'Maybe so. But the odds of dying in bed are in your favor.'

'Now you sound like Ellie. Always begging me to find a job that doesn't make her worry 'bout me getting shot all the time.'

'Not the worst idea she's ever had.'

'Maybe not. But I can't oblige her. Not and still piss standing up.'

'Being a man means being responsible, that it?'

'No one's said it better.'

'Even if it means losing Ellie?'

His tight-lipped silence told me yes. I didn't know what else to say.

'You figure I'm *loco*, right?'

I shrugged. 'What I figure don't matter.'

'Does to me.'

'Okay. Then: no, I don't think you're *loco*. I think you've finally turned the corner.'

'Meaning?'

'Made an important decision all by your lonesome.'

''Bout time, wouldn't you say?'

'That's for true.'

Heck shook his head in mock disgust. 'Now you're stealing my words as well as my woman.'

'Women,' I corrected. 'Marley's already left her shoes under my bed.'

'I hope you mean that figuratively?'

'If I don't, I've just taken my first step back to prison.'

We both laughed; more, I think, to ease the tension rather than because we were happy.

'Listen,' I said, 'you know I'm not one to get emotional. But right now, Little Brother, I'm as proud of you as I've ever been. And much as I love

Ellie, I love you more. And no matter how things eventually turn out, I got your back, just like I know you got mine.'

Heck swallowed a lump before saying gruffly: 'Thanks, *hermano*. That means more to me than you'll ever know.' For a moment he stared at the shotgun as if it had all the answers. Then he smiled at me, said, 'See you soon,' and continued on along Hell Street.

'See you soon,' I replied. Turning, I started walking in the direction of the cabin.

Off in the distance there was more shooting.

It didn't come from the same direction as Heck was headed, but for some unknown reason I felt the hairs on the back of my neck prickle. I was tempted to turn around and go after Heck. Before I could, I heard more shooting.

There were six shots altogether. And this time they *did* come from the direction Heck had taken. They were followed by a deadly silence that chilled my blood. Because even before I'd whirled around and started running after my brother, I knew Heck was dead.

# 8

I found him lying face-down in the dirt in front of the Texas Saloon. There were four bullet holes in his back. Several men I didn't recognize were standing around him, staring at the body as if they couldn't believe Heck had been shot.

One of them shook his head at me as I came running up, indicating that my brother was dead.

Hoping he was wrong I knelt beside Heck, gently rolled him over, pressed my ear against his chest and listened for a pulse. There wasn't one. Just like that my brother was gone. Forever. Something cold and clammy dropped in my belly. Simultaneously, a white-hot rage surged through me. I looked at the men. 'Any of you see who shot him?'

Two of them shook their heads.

A third man said: 'Three men. I didn't see their faces but one of 'em was riding a pinto, you know, like the one Bryce Guthrie rides.'

'You saying the Guthries shot my brother?'

The three men exchanged looks and then one of them shrugged.

'Seems reasonable, marshal,' he said.

The same tall young cowboy with bleary eyes that I'd seen earlier in the saloon, took a swig from a half-empty bottle of tequila, swayed drunkenly for a moment and then said: 'S'more than reasonable, deputy. Hell, I'd bet a dollar to a bent nickel it was one of the Guthrie brothers.'

I straightened up, almost as tall as the young cowboy now, asking: 'What makes you say that?'

''Cause earlier they was standing next to me at the bar and I heard 'em talking 'bout how they was going to take care of your brother and then high-tail it for Mexico.'

'Not Albuquerque?' I said, remembering what he'd told Heck in the saloon.

'Uh-uh. Sure as I'm standing here, they said the border — ' He paused, as if puzzled by my question, and then added: 'I know I said Albuquerque before, mister, 'cause that's what they said then. But this time these boys definitely said Mexico.'

'Thanks,' I said. I dug out a silver dollar and flipped it to him. 'Next one's on me.'

'Why, thanks, mister. That's mighty white of you.'

I hunkered down, slipped one arm under my brother's back, the other under his legs and then straightened up. He felt weightless in my arms and holding him like a newborn calf, I began walking in the direction of the cabin.

I was sick inside. Not so much with grief, though there was plenty of that as well, but with an all-consuming rage that I knew would never go away until I'd killed the Guthrie brothers and left their bodies to be picked clean by vultures.

# 9

That night, with the help of the moon, we buried Heck on the scrub-covered slope behind the cabin. It was a good place to be buried. It overlooked the canyon and the distant mountains, a view Ellie said my brother especially enjoyed at sunset, when the rays of the setting sun reddened the slope, warming the dirt so that even the dead would not feel the chill of falling dusk each evening.

Worried that the outlaws who hated Heck might dig up his corpse and drag it through town, as they had the last two marshals they'd killed, we decided not to tell anyone where he was buried. Not even the undertaker. Instead, I dug the grave myself, placed my brother's gun and gun-belt atop the coffin, after which Ellie and Marley tearfully read a few comforting verses from the Bible.

We then lowered the coffin into the hole and I shoveled dirt over it. As if nature itself felt Heck's loss, clouds respectfully covered the moon and it became so dark, we needed the oil lamp to find our way back to the cabin.

There, Ellie put Marley to bed, staying with her until she had cried herself to sleep. Meanwhile, I made fresh coffee and when Ellie returned, we sat across the table from each other, neither of us saying anything, just sipping our coffee in grim silence.

Every now and then Ellie set her cup down and wiped away her tears with a dainty, lace-edged handkerchief that had her initials embroidered in one corner. Once, when she caught me watching her, she stopped twisting and untwisting the handkerchief around her finger and felt obliged to say, in a sad little girl's voice that seemed to come from far-off:

'I suppose you think I'm silly.'

'Silly?'

'For bringing all my possessions with

me from home?'

'Why would I think that?'

'Heck did.'

'I'm not Heck.'

As if I hadn't spoken, she said: 'But then, much as he loved me, he never understood what they meant to me.'

'How do you know that?'

'From things he said over the years.' She gazed at the once-elegant-now-battered furniture. 'Though he'd never admit it, I think he felt threatened by them.'

'Threatened?'

'Yes, especially by my keepsakes. Of course he always denied it whenever I brought it up, but I knew better. I could tell he was jealous of them.'

'That doesn't sound like Heck, Ellie.'

'Maybe you didn't know him as well as you think?'

I doubted that but let it slide. 'Why would he be jealous?'

'Because he thought they stole a part of me away from him.'

'Aw, c'mon.'

'I'm serious.' She paused and stared at the damp, twisted handkerchief. 'In a strange way, I suppose he was right.'

'I don't follow.'

'By their very presence they kept my childhood memories alive, along with my love for my family. Heck didn't like that.'

'Why?'

'Because, God love him, he was very possessive and wanted me all to himself. And he knew that as long as I had my things around me, my memories would remain fresh and vivid, preventing him from owning every part of me.'

I found it hard to believe that Heck was so possessive. Hell, I knew him as well if not better than anyone and not once had he ever mentioned feeling that way about Ellie or any other woman.

As if reading my mind, she said: 'Why would I make something like that up?'

'Beats me.'

'I wouldn't and you of all people

know I wouldn't,' she said crossly.

I had to admit she was right. In all the years I'd known her, I couldn't remember her lying. I studied her tear-streaked face, still trying to digest the idea that Heck was overly possessive and at the same time wondering if she was hinting that I had a dark side too.

'Listen,' I said finally, 'I'm not saying you're right or wrong about Heck. That's something only you and he know for true. But as God is my witness, during the time we were together I never felt that way about you or your belongings ... or, for that matter, your past.'

'I know. But Heck isn't — wasn't you. He was a good man, a fine man ... and in many ways a better man for me than you, but the love I felt for you went deeper. And I think he sensed that ... though he was too much of a gentleman to ever throw it in my face.' She paused, fighting back tears that threatened to overwhelm her, then said: 'This isn't the time or place to go into how much I loved you, Lute, or missed you when you left me. I hurt way too much right now . . . and I'm sure you do too.'

I nodded. I had so much to say to her, but the pain of Heck's loss all but consumed me, so I held my silence. I also felt guilty about my feelings for Ellie with my brother's death still so vivid in my mind.

'Later,' Ellie said as if reading my mind, 'once it's fully sunk in that I've lost Heck forever, and I don't feel so damned guilty for still loving you, we'll talk about this some more. But until then . . . ' Her voice, choked with tears, tailed off.

'I understand,' I said.

We were both silent for several moments. Neither of us seemed to know how to break the growing silence.

Finally, I stood up, said: 'Reckon I'll go to bed now.'

'Me, too,' Ellie said. Tears flooded her eyes and she lowered her head so I wouldn't see them. 'Though I don't know why. I very much doubt that I'll get any sleep.'

'If it would help, I'll gladly stay here for the night.'

'Thanks, but I'll manage . . . ' Ellie smiled through her tears, leaned close and kissed me on the forehead. 'Good night, dear Lute.'

'G'night,' I said. I watched as she turned and sadly walked into the bedroom.

Inside, it felt like someone had snatched out my heart.

# 10

I'd intended to set out after the Guthrie brothers as soon as Ellie went to bed. But while we were burying my brother she begged me to wait until morning, so I could further comfort Marley and reassure her that her world had not ended with her father's death. I agreed, at the same time sensing that although Ellie hadn't mentioned it, she wanted me there to give her moral support too.

Since it was almost dawn anyway, I didn't bother to use the mattress in the shed but continued to sit there at the table, smoking one hand-rolled after another, drinking the last of the coffee and struggling to accept the grim reality of my brother's death.

The night dragged slowly by. I don't remember falling asleep, but I must have because the next thing I remembered was waking up and realizing I was slumped over the table. I rubbed the sleep from my eyes, yawned, rose and went outside. It was clear and cold and a sharp breeze off the canyon made me shiver. Dawn was approaching. The pale gray sky was flooded with streaks of yellow, green, pink and violet. I went to the pump, removed my shirt and splashed cold water over my body until I was wide awake. Then, skin tingling, I returned inside the cabin and made a fresh pot of coffee.

I was standing at the stove, savoring the aroma, when Marley joined me. Still in her nightgown, she was barefoot, her long sun-streaked hair hung over her face and her eyes were raw from crying and full of sleep.

'G'morning,' I said.

''Morning, Uncle Lute.' She took two mugs from a cupboard and brought them to the table. I'd never known her to drink coffee before and must have looked surprised because as she sat down, she said: 'It's all right, Uncle Lute, momma doesn't mind.'

'When'd you start drinking coffee?' I asked, filling her mug.

'Oh, ages ago . . . '

I sensed she was lying, but figured one mug of coffee couldn't hurt her. I watched as she blew on the coffee to cool it and then took a sip that made her grimace. 'Urgh. No wonder people put lots of sugar in it.'

'Condensed milk works just as well,' I suggested.

'Really? I bet that's why Momma always keeps plenty of it in the pantry.' Rising, Marley took a can of condensed milk from a cupboard and brought it back to the table. 'It's already been opened. See?' She pointed at the two little holes punched in the top.

'Take it easy,' I said as she poured condensed milk into her coffee. 'It's mighty sweet. Too much kills the taste of the coffee.'

She gave me a look as if to say she already knew that, but stopped pouring and stirred her coffee before taking a sip. 'Mm-mm, that's much better. Want some, Uncle Lute?'

'Uh-uh. Blacker the better for me.' I gulped down a mouthful of hot coffee.

'Doesn't that burn, Uncle Lute? I mean, it's awful hot.'

'When you've drunk as much range coffee as I have, missy, made by cooks whose one goal in life is to poison you, the roof of your mouth soon loses all sense of feeling.'

Marley eyed me suspiciously. 'Is that another of your tall tales, Uncle Lute?'

'Uh-uh. It's pure Gospel.'

Not convinced, she took another cautious sip of coffee. I glimpsed tears in her eyes and sensed she was about to start weeping. A woman crying, no matter their age, is something I've never been able to handle and I was determined to stop Marley at all costs.

'Listen,' I said, 'while we're alone, missy, there's something I want to tell you.'

'You're going after the men who killed daddy?'

I nodded. 'Soon as your mom wakes up.'

'Good. Promise me that when you catch them you won't let them live. You won't, will you?' she said when I didn't answer.

'Don't worry, missy. The Guthries will never see the inside of a jail or a courtroom.'

Satisfied, Marley sipped her coffee, eyes burning with hate. 'Wish I could go with you, Uncle Lute. I know it's a dreadful thing to say, and momma would scold me for it, but I'd give anything to be the one who pulled the trigger.'

'I'm sure you would. What's more, I don't blame you. But you got a more important job to do — '

'What's more important than killing the men who shot my dad?'

'Nothing. But that's my job. Yours is to look after your mom while I'm gone.'

'Don't you mean the other way 'round?'

'Normally I would, yeah. But you're

different. Special. Age-wise, you may only be fourteen or fifteen or whatever you are, but mentally you're way beyond your years.'

Marley cocked her head and eyed me doubtfully. 'You really mean that, Uncle Lute?'

'Absolutely. What's more, your pa felt the same way. Told me so, many times. Said you were one of the most responsible people he knew — young or old — and if anything ever happened to him, I was to treat you like a grownup.'

'Really?' Marley wiped her eyes and brightened. 'Well, I sure try to be responsible, Uncle Lute. I just never thought daddy noticed. Him or momma.'

'They noticed, missy, believe me. So have I. That's why I'm trusting you to do as I ask. Can you do that for me?' I asked as she yawned again.

'If you think momma needs me to, sure.'

'I do. Remember this, Marley: the next few weeks are going to be mighty tough on her. She's not only going to miss my brother as a husband — which is painful and stressful enough — she has to take on the added responsibility of being both mom and dad to you, and that's no joke. From now on, she's got to worry about how she's going to look after you, feed you, support you, make sure get a good schooling — all those kinds of things. Things which Heck would've helped her with, leaving her more time to spend with you.'

Marley frowned, said: 'You know, Uncle Lute, I never thought of it that way.'

'Understandable. Losing someone you love hurts so much that for a while it's all you can think of. Believe me, I know. Both Heck and me, we lost our folks when we were real young, and had no one in the world but each other.'

'But you made it all right.'

'You bet. And so will you and your mom. I just don't want her to have to shoulder the whole load alone while I'm gone, that's all. Not when she's got you to help her.'

Marley nodded. The tears I'd seen earlier had now disappeared and in their place was the same gritty determination that I'd always admired in Heck. 'You needn't worry, Uncle Lute. I'll never let you down — you or momma.'

'Hell, I know that. I just needed to convince you.' I leaned across the table and kissed her on the forehead. 'Oh, and one other thing: let this be our little secret, okay?'

''Mean don't tell momma?'

'Her or anyone else you talk to.'

'All right. I won't tell a soul. I'll just look after her, like you want, until you get back. You *are* coming, aren't you?' she added, suddenly concerned. 'After you've killed the Guthrie brothers, I mean?'

'I'll sure try,' I said, not wanting to make a promise I might have to break.

'You better do better than that,' a voice said behind me.

I turned and saw Ellie, wearing a robe, eyes raw from crying, standing in the doorway.

'You don't want to miss little Heck, Jr's christening, do you?'

'Heck, Jr?' I repeated.

'Sure. You're his only uncle, you know. You've got to be there.'

'Oh, I'll be there,' I assured. 'No matter if it's a Heck or a Helen.'

'I just told you,' Ellie said almost crossly. 'It's going to be a boy.'

'How can you be so sure? Hell, I don't know much about babies, but isn't it a mite early yet to know if it's going to be a colt or a filly?'

Ellie patted her slightly swollen belly and smiled as if she knew a secret. 'Under normal circumstances, yes. But this pregnancy isn't normal.'

Marley looked alarmed. 'W-What do you mean, momma? You're not sick, are you?'

''Course not, sweetheart. I'm strong as a horse.'

'Then how do you know it's going to be a boy?' I said.

Ellie hesitated, as if not sure whether she should tell me. Then she said: 'Well, if you promise not to laugh, I'll tell you. Ever since I've been with child, I've had this recurring dream. In it I'm always giving birth and the baby is always a boy.'

Marley's eyes widened. 'Is that for true, momma? Am I really going to have a baby brother?'

'That's what I'm expecting, sweetheart, yes. You're going to have a baby brother.'

Marley gave a squeal of delight. 'Oh, momma!' she exclaimed, rising and hugging Ellie. 'I can't believe it. All these years, I've prayed and prayed that you and daddy would have another baby, and it would be a boy. Now my prayers are finally going to come true!'

I caught Ellie looking at me over her daughter's shoulder. She smiled, eyes brimming with tears of happiness, her expression a mixture of heartache and joy.

I smiled back at her, thinking now that everything was going to turn out all right for her and Marley.

I went to the door and motioned that I was going out to saddle up.

'Before you ride off,' Ellie said, 'I'll fix you some ham and eggs. You most likely got a long hard ride ahead of you and I don't want you doing it on an empty stomach.'

I started to protest, but she had already turned away from Marley and was stirring last night's embers in the stove.

'Thanks,' I told her. 'Much obliged.'

'Marley,' Ellie said, 'go out and fetch me some more kindling, please.'

'Yes, momma. Right away.'

She looked at me. We both winked at each other, and then together left the cabin.

# 11

After I'd eaten breakfast and said my goodbyes, I rode to Dawson's Livery and put a bridle on Heck's grullo mare, Chloe. I left my brother's saddle with the liveryman, promising to pick it up on my return. Mounting, I urged my horse forward and led the skittish, silvery-white mare out of the stable.

Though wild and dangerous at night, Canyon Diablo was almost a ghost town during the day. Now, with dawn lingering, the only folks on Hell Street were the drunks sleeping it off outside the various saloons. I rode past them and followed the trail out of town, south toward the border.

It was several hundred miles to Mexico. Since the Guthries had gotten a jump on me, I pushed the horses hard. I wasn't worried about my sorrel. Cisco was bred for endurance and over the years had outlasted every posse that had pursued me. I wasn't so sure about the grullo. But the sturdy little mare surprised me. Despite being afraid of her own shadow, after two hours Chloe was still reasonably fresh, so I rode her for another hour and then rested briefly before changing horses.

I had no idea how close I was to the Guthrie brothers. It would have been easier on me if one of their horses' shoes was loose or had marks I could recognize, as they always did in Ned Buntline's dime novels, but no such luck. There were countless hoof prints in the dirt, any of which could have belonged to the Guthries' horses. My only hope of tracking them down was if they were headed for Mexico, like the tall young cowboy told me, because then this would be the trail they took.

I rode until the horses became weary. I didn't see any towns, but passed through three small settlements comprised of tents and shacks, stores and makeshift saloons. By the looks of the gaunt, raggedy-dressed families living there, I figured they were barely eking out a living. They stared curiously at me as I rode past, especially the young'uns, and then returned to their chores. I stopped in each settlement and asked several people if they had seen three riders fitting the Guthrie brothers' description. Nobody had. One gnarly old miner, who was panning for gold in one of the streams I rode across, grabbed his Confederate muzzle-loading rifle and threatened to shoot me if I came any closer.

'Don't sweat it, old-timer,' I said, flashing my Deputy U.S. Marshal's badge. 'I'm not after your dust. I'm tracking three men who might have ridden through here in the past day or two.'

'Ain't *nobody* ridden past me,' he replied, still wary of me. 'And I been panning in this creek from dawn till dusk for nigh on six months.'

Thanking him, I rode on. I was now in red dirt country, surrounded by scrub-covered hills and sandstone cliffs that changed from bright orange to crimson when the sun hit them. The trail led through steep-walled canyons and over rocky slopes, and occasionally past stands of stumpy, parched oak trees that often were parched and leafless.

It was now late afternoon and I still hadn't seen any trace of the Guthrie brothers. I wondered if they were pushing their horses equally hard or in order to avoid being caught they'd taken a different, longer trail to the border. Either way I doubted if I could overtake them before dark and decided to make camp and take up the chase at sunrise.

From what other convicts had told me, there was only one legitimate town in this part of the territory. Though it wasn't as big as Tucson, they said it was growing rapidly, with stores, hotels, saloons, brothels, gambling parlors and houses sprouting up everywhere as if the town was trying to justify the meaning of its mythological name, Phoenix.

Hopefully, I thought as I fed the horses a handful of grain each then let them chew on the weeds by a shallow creek, the Guthries would be tempted to stay in town overnight to revel in the whorehouses and cantinas, enabling me to catch up with them tomorrow. If not, then I'd follow them into Mexico and hunt them down in one of the many lawless villages along the border.

First though I had to eat. Building a fire beside the creek, I fried some bacon and beans and ate them out of the skillet. Then I stretched out on my bedroll, rolled myself a smoke, flared a match and leaned back against my saddle. As I smoked and stared at the stars I wondered why someone as decent and honorable as Heck, with so much to live for, had to die when I, who other than reading every book in the prison library — including the encyclo-pedias — had made no significant contribution to life, seemed to possess a cat's proverbial nine lives.

It was a question that had haunted me ever since my brother's death. It grew worse at night, making sleep almost impossible. But fortunately tonight I was so exhausted I dozed off before I could torture myself too badly with guilt.

# 12

I reached Phoenix by mid-morning the next day. The convicts were right: I'd never seen so much building going on at once. The whole town seemed to be rising out of the desert all around me. Everywhere workmen were busy as ants. Their hammering and sawing drowned out the noise of the riders and horse-drawn traffic moving up and down Washington Street, a broad dirt thoroughfare running through the center of downtown.

As I rode along among the traffic, head swiveling to take in all the finished and half-finished stores, saloons, dance halls and shaded gambling tables offering faro and Three-Card Monte games, I noticed a large, newly-erected adobe building on the corner of 2nd Avenue and Washington Street. It had a cross atop the roof and a sign outside the front door that read: Central Methodist Church.

I hadn't been to church since my folks passed, and for a moment I felt a strange urge to go in and say a prayer for Ellie and Marley. I fought it down, fearing that once inside I'd be too embarrassed to pray, and rode on.

It was fortunate I did. For ahead I saw several horses tied up outside the Tiger Saloon. Among them stood a leggy gray with a fancy black saddle that looked familiar. I was trying to remember where I'd seen it before when a man emerged from the saloon. He was as lean and hard-bellied as a desert rider, and his clothes were caked with sweat and dust. He paused on the red-brick sidewalk to light a cigar. He tilted his head back slightly as he inspected the now-burning tip and in that instant I recognized his bearded face: it was the youngest of the Guthrie brothers, Bryce.

I reined up sharply, wondering as I did if his brothers, Doke and Gibby, were inside the saloon. There was one way to find out. I drew my Colt and spurred my horse forward, guiding Cisco and the mare between the wagons, buckboards and riders blocking my path to the saloon.

Bryce didn't see me coming. He took a long pull on the cigar and then contentedly exhaled the smoke through pursed lips. I was close now and could have shot him easily. But I knew that wouldn't satisfy me. I wanted to look into his eyes, to see the shock and the pain in them as he felt my slug rip through him, so I held my fire.

It was a costly mistake. For in the next moment Bryce must have heard my horse coming and turned toward me. He instantly recognized me and in one continuous move whirled around and dived through the saloon swing-doors.

I didn't bother to dismount. Dropping the mare's reins, so I wasn't hampered by her, I spurred my horse onto the red-brick sidewalk and without stopping, ducked my head and rode into the saloon.

A dozen shots greeted me. I heard Cisco grunt and knew he'd been hit. By then I had spotted the Guthrie brothers firing around the sides of upturned tables, and opened fire on them. I saw the oldest brother, Doke, grab his arm up by his shoulder and spin around, while my other shots forced Gibby and Bryce to pull back behind their tables.

By now the panicked customers had scattered in different directions and both barkeeps had ducked below the bar. But they weren't safe there. A wild shot smashed the mirror above the back-bar and shards of glass showered over them. The tall red-faced bartender was cut on the cheek by the falling glass and blood spattered over his soiled white apron.

I had troubles of my own. Beneath me Cisco now collapsed to his knees, snorting and squealing in pain. Blood-flecked foam sprayed from the sorrel's mouth and I knew death was only moments away. With no time to dismount, I jumped from the saddle and dived behind the end of the bar. There, I hunched down, bullets whining about my head, and quickly reloaded. On the floor beside me Cisco kicked spasmodically for a few moments, shuddered, and lay still.

There wasn't time to feel sorry about losing my horse. Peering around the end of the bar I saw Gibby's head poking over the upturned table and fired a quick shot. The bullet tore off the top of his ear and he fell back screaming. I continued firing at the table he was hiding behind. But the table was solid oak and the bullets ricocheted in all directions. One of them shattered the glittering crystal chandelier hanging from the ceiling. It swung back and forth, dangerously close to dropping, pieces of broken crystal raining down on customers hiding behind tables below. Yelps and curses came from them.

Suddenly Gibby and Bryce made a break for the door leading to the kitchen. I snapped off a shot. It missed, and when I pulled the trigger again all I heard was a dull click. Swearing, I hunkered down and started to reload. That's when I heard a louder, more ominous double-click as someone thumbed back twin hammers. I'd heard that sound before. It froze my blood and even as I looked up, I knew what I'd see before I actually saw it: the side-by-side barrels of a shotgun pointing at me from a few feet away.

'Drop it, mister,' the red-faced barkeep said.

'I'm a Deputy U.S. Marshal,' I began.

He cut me off. 'Can be Jesus Christ Hisself for all I care, mister. But if you don't drop that iron, I'll paint the wall with you.' He prodded me with the scattergun and I quickly dropped my Colt.

'Now stand up,' he ordered.

I obeyed, hands raised, the saloon suddenly so quiet I could hear my heart thud-thudding. Then, slowly, cautiously, customers began emerging from behind cover.

Out the corner of my eye I saw the Guthrie brothers stand up, guns aimed at me.

'Thanks, Cap,' Doke said. 'We'll take over from here.'

'Hold it!' the other barkeep barked. He was almost as wide as he was tall and his stubby fingers were so fat he could barely curl them around the triggers of the sawed-off he was aiming at the brothers. 'There'll be no more blood spilled here.'

'Suit yourself,' Doke said. Blood stained his shirt where I'd shot him and every movement made him wince. 'We'll take the sonofabitch outside and kill him there.'

The red-faced barkeep turned to me. 'What you just said — 'bout being a deputy marshal — that true?'

One-handed, I pulled back my jacket to show the badge pinned on my shirt.

He leaned close and squinted at it, as

if nearsighted, then lowered his shot-gun.

'Go ahead, marshal. Pick up your gun.'

I obeyed. I moved slowly, so as not to make him nervous, and holstered my Colt.

'What now?' I asked.

'Take it outside,' the other barkeep said. When the Guthrie brothers didn't move, he wagged the sawed-off shotgun at them, adding: 'That means all of you!'

There was no arguing with that scattergun. Keeping my eyes on the brothers, I backed out of the saloon. The Guthries didn't follow and I figured they ducked out the rear door. There wasn't much I could do to stop them. I looked around for Heck's grullo and saw the mare standing nearby, impatiently swishing her long black tail. Now all I needed was my saddle and rifle.

Just then, as if he'd been reading my mind, the red-faced bartender looked over the batwing doors at me. 'Wallen-kamp's Livery is just down the block,' he said, blinking as sweat stung his eyes. 'Ask for Brent and tell him Cap sent you. He's got a wagon and a winch. 'Bout the only way you're going to get your horse out of here.'

'Much obliged,' I said, and hurried off toward the stables.

# 13

After I'd paid Brent Wallenkamp to drag away the dead sorrel and bury it in the desert, I saddled the mare and rode around behind the saloon. For once luck was with me. There were three sets of hoof prints in the dirt near the back door. Guessing that they belonged to the Guthrie brothers' horses, I dismounted and hunkered down to examine them. There was nothing unusual about two of the sets, but one of the shoes belonging to the third set had a small v-shaped crack on the left side. Now, like one of Ned Buntline's heroes, I had something to go on and could track the Guthries until a new shoe was nailed on.

Tracking was a challenging, laborious process, especially since my eyesight was far from perfect. I had to hold the mare to a slow easy lope, stopping every half-mile or so to dismount and examine the ground to make sure the cracked horseshoe print was still visible. It was damned frustrating. Every time I stopped I knew the Guthrie brothers were getting farther away from me. The mare didn't make it any easier. She wanted to run and tugged impatiently at the bit when I kept her reined in. And each time I stopped to verify the prints she impatiently stamped the ground with her left foreleg as if urging me to hurry up and get on with the chase.

I liked her feistiness. It helped make up for her skittishness. And though I missed Cisco and was sorry he'd died in such an ugly way, the mare soon endeared herself to me, making it easier to handle his loss.

*　*　*

I covered forty miles that day. That meant I had another two days' ride before I reached the border. Even more disconcerting was the fact that I was now deep in Apache territory and could expect no mercy if I was caught. I'd seen no smoke signals or mirror flashes relaying messages from one lookout to the next, but that didn't mean I wasn't being watched. I almost certainly was. With Cochise dead, the various tribes were no longer banded together but were now ruled individually by boastful young warriors and sub-chiefs who fought amongst themselves almost as much as they fought the whites. But they still sent out roving bands to patrol their territory, and I knew that if I was spotted by one of them I'd be chased and, if caught, dragged back to camp. There I'd be beaten by the squaws, then staked out over an anthill until I was barely alive and finally used for target practice or slowly burned to death.

It was a chilling thought and that night I chose my camp very carefully, making sure that I was protected on three sides by rocks. I then hobbled the mare near my bedroll and wove a fence out of thorn bushes which I used to block the last open side. It was too risky to build a fire, so I ate beef jerky and hardtack and washed everything down with water. By that time I was so damned tired, I fell asleep almost as soon as I got under my blanket.

The next morning I woke before sunup. I wasted no time fixing breakfast or boiling water for coffee, but saddled the mare before dawn broke and started for the border. It was cold, as only the desert can get cold, and despite my heavy coat I'd ridden several miles before I quit shivering. By then dawn had chased the stars away and the pale gray sky was aflame with brilliant colors. I hardly noticed. At this point I was more concerned with keeping my hair than admiring sunrises or even finding the Guthrie brothers, so I stopped looking for prints and pushed the mare hard. She responded, almost joyfully, and mile after mile fell behind us.

Every hour or so I reined up, dismounted and loosened the cinch to give the mare a breather. There was plenty of cover to hide us from Apache lookouts, but whether it was a rocky outcrop, dry riverbed or ravine the fear of being spotted never left my mind and by midday my jaw ached from unconsciously gritting my teeth. From then on I kept a wad of chewing tobacco in my mouth, constantly shifting it from cheek to cheek in order to keep my jaw relaxed.

It was late afternoon when I saw my first smoke signal. It was off in the distance and I didn't think it had anything to do with me, but to be on the safe side I quickly took cover behind a stand of dead, sun-bleached oaks. From there I watched through my field glasses as the puffs of white smoke rose intermittently from the distant hilltop. The signal only lasted a few minutes and though I scanned every peak, cliff and hill on the horizon, I never saw any response to the message.

I waited another ten minutes or so, just to be sure, and then continued riding south. I hadn't gone more than a mile when I noticed something moving along the ridge to my right. I immediately reigned up, dismounted and led the mare behind three giant saguaro cactuses. Easily thirty feet tall, with upthrust arms reaching even higher, they stood side-by-side like green-clad sentinels atop a low rock-strewn mound. Dwarfed by them, I dug out my glasses and trained them on the ridge.

As I screwed the eyepieces around, suddenly a dozen or more Apaches armed with rifles leaped into focus. They were wearing war paint and so were the ponies they were leading. They weren't in any hurry, and showed no sign of having seen me, but I still felt a clammy shiver crawl up my spine. Beside me the mare had no such qualms. Anxious to move on, she kept stamping her foreleg and nudging me with her nose. I cursed her softly and gripped the reins firmly in case she decided to dart out from behind the cactuses.

The Apaches had reached the end of the ridge. Swinging up onto the bare backs of their ponies, they rode down the steep slope to the base of the ridge, now no more than a half-mile away. I watched them for a few more moments then realized they were headed toward me. I pulled my rifle from its boot, levered in a round and waited tensely to see if the braves continued to ride my way. They did. I began to sweat. Though the giant cactuses provided enough cover to keep me hidden from them at their present distance, I knew that once they got closer they would spot me. And since they were on the warpath, I knew they'd surely try to kill or capture me.

I looked around, wondering if I could find a better place to make a stand. But all about me the desert was flat except for a scattering of rocky outcrops on my left. They weren't too far away and might have offered protection, but they were all too steep to climb, so I wrote them off and prepared to defend myself if attacked.

The Apaches were now no more than a hundred yards from me. They still hadn't seen me, which was a miracle in itself, but I knew it was only a matter of moments before they did. I dropped the reins, hoping the mare wouldn't wander off, pressed my rifle against my cheek and lined the sights up on the nearest brave. I figured I could drop him and two or three others before they knew what hit them, and perhaps another two in the ensuing shootout. But that still left six I had to contend with at close quarters — and though I'm fully capable of protecting myself with pistol and Bowie knife, I still hated the odds.

I watched the Apaches riding closer, always keeping the leader in my sights, knowing that any moment now I was going to end his life. I've killed many men in my time, most of them close enough to see the fear in their eyes, but it never gets any easier. Each death adds a scar to my conscience, and though I'd never killed a man who wasn't intent on killing me, that justification had long ago stopped making me feel better about myself.

The lead Apache, a short bulky man with white war paint beneath his dark savage eyes, was now only fifty yards from me. I knew any second he'd spot me and was curling my finger around the trigger, ready to shoot him, when shots rang out.

They came from the direction of the rocky outcrops. Surprised, I turned and saw some twenty odd braves burst out from behind the rocks. They were all on foot, firing as they ran. They were a ragtag bunch. Some of them wore U.S. Cavalry tunics that didn't fit them, others settlers' clothing, while one brave wore a yellow woman's dress over his shirt. All the clothes were blood-stained, suggesting they'd taken them off dead bodies. If that wasn't enough to make any white man's blood boil, the warriors were also armed with stolen military carbines and single-action revolvers, and were deadly accurate with both.

I was so furious I almost shot the heathen bastards. But I knew if I did it would only betray my position, so I controlled myself and waited to see how the battle turned out.

The mounted Apaches hadn't a chance. Caught off-guard by the sudden attack, several of them were killed immediately, while the others milled around in panic, preventing any of them from getting off clean shots.

The blood bath was over in minutes. The attacking Apaches closed in, whooping and shouting, and quickly scalped their victims. Some of the victims were still alive and their agonizing screams as their scalps were cut off made me wince. I've seen plenty of men and women scalped before, and others tortured in hideously cruel ways, so it shouldn't have bothered me. But something about the pure savage enjoyment the Apaches exuded as they butchered their enemies turned my stomach.

Finally the scalping ended. The joyous, blood-spattered victors swung up onto their enemies' ponies, scalps draped around their necks, and rode off.

Relieved, I stood there, reliving the scene I'd just witnessed. Then, angry with myself for letting it affect me, I tucked my rifle into the saddle-boot, stepped up into the saddle and grasped the reins. That's when I realized my hands were trembling. It was a new experience. Troubled by it and cursing myself for being a weak-kneed sister, I kicked up the mare and headed for the border.

# 14

It took another day of hard riding to reach Mexico. Dusk was falling as I crossed the border. But there was still some daylight left, and after a lengthy search I found several groups of hoof prints in the sandy dirt. Unfortunately, none of them had a v-shaped crack.

Frustrated, I kicked a stone that skidded past the mare, startling her. She reared up, snorting to show she was angry with me. I ignored her, which pissed her off even more. She edged closer. Certain that she meant to either kick or bite me, I quickly jumped back. That really got her goat and she bared her teeth at me.

I sensed she was bluffing, but kept out of her way anyway. I filled my canteen at a waterhole that had been there as long as I could remember and let the mare drink until she'd quenched her thirst. I then fed her the last handful of oats. While she ate them, I sat on a rock and crunched down a piece of hardtack. High above me I heard a screech and, looking up, saw a bat falcon circling overhead. I'm not one who kills for pleasure, but sometimes frustration gets the better of me and before I knew it my Colt was in my hand and I'd snapped off a shot at the falcon. The bullet was close enough to cut off a few tail feathers, scaring the bird away.

I realized then what a foul mood I was in. I desperately wanted to kill the Guthrie brothers, and to be this close to them yet not know where they were was driving me *loco*. I sensed the sonsofbitches were slipping away from me and knew that I had to nail them now or risk losing them for maybe weeks, months or even longer. Because, God knows I'm not a great tracker. I knew if I couldn't find the cracked hoof print now there was no telling how long it might take before I picked up the

Guthries' trail again. But though I carefully searched the ground in every direction, I still couldn't find a trace of the cracked-shoe print. I was stumped and losing light fast.

To calm myself rolled a smoke, lit it and took a drag. The smoke hit my lungs and I held it there a moment, savoring the taste, and then exhaled. I immediately felt better. I finished the cigarette and feeling more relaxed, let my mind wander.

It was then it hit me. I was familiar with this part of the country, having often hidden out here to avoid bounty hunters and lawmen that were anxious to see me hang, and it suddenly dawned on me there was a pueblo about a mile away. Built around the old abandoned Spanish mission of San Cristobal, it was too insignificant to be on the map. But it had two cantinas that were popular with outlaws and border trash. Both places had willing whores and a back room that could be rented for a few pesos, and knowing the Guthrie brothers' insatiable appetite for sex and whisky I took a chance that they would hole up there for a day or two and guided the weary-but-still-game mare east.

This part of Mexico was particularly wild and rugged. Everywhere there were canyons, untamed rivers, deserts and rocky hills that served as nature's stepping stones to the mighty Sierra Madre Occidental. The mountains were home to bands of ruthless bandits, known as *Bandidos de las Montanas*. They robbed and killed anyone they came across without fear of reprisal from either the local police, whom they bribed, or the woefully inadequate *Rurales*. Before going to prison I'd had several run-ins with the *Rurales*. They were fine horsemen who looked splendid in their gray uniforms, silver braid and shiny buttons as they rode about the territory, but as mounted policemen they were a public embarrassment. They were poorly trained, undisciplined, lazy and easily corrupted.

Worse, they used their authority to bully parents into forcing their daughters to sleep with them, which made the villagers despise them.

But who cared? This was Mexico, a country ruled by ruthless greedy despots who got fat on corruption. They took what they wanted, when they wanted it, and killed anyone who protested. Was it any wonder then that others with authority below them acted the same way?

As one old *pistolero* once said to me: 'What else can you expect, *amigo*, when you conscript lowly farmers, crop pickers and *campesinos* from local villages, whose relatives are bandits themselves?' I agreed with him. In all fairness though, what he failed to mention was that the *Rurales* were paid next to nothing and shunned by villagers who'd once been their friends. Also, their folks' lives were in constant danger from villagers seeking revenge for a raped daughter or stolen food, so it wasn't surprising that they were frequently deserting and always had their hand out.

They'd demanded money from me on several occasions and I'd always turned them down. This meant I couldn't expect any help from them. Up till now I hadn't needed it. But now in order to get to San Cristobal I had to cross the northern tip of the Sonoran Desert, a vast forbidding area that stretched for hundreds of miles along the border and was famous for its splendor, giant saguaro cactuses and deadly bandit attacks. The bandits were especially dangerous at night, when they not only stole from sleeping travelers but slit their throats just for the hell of it. Deciding not to take that risk, I made sure the mare was watered and well-rested and then rode across the barren scrubland in the moonlight.

I rode all night, stopping only when I felt the mare needed a breather, and by dawn had reached the outskirts of San Cristobal. I reined up behind some rocks, got out my field glasses and studied the shabby little village. Other than crowing roosters nothing was stirring. I raised my glasses. Above the red-tiled rooftops of the white-washed adobe-brick dwellings that lined both sides of the main street I could see the tall square bell tower of the mission. A swarm of bats darted about the tower, hunting insects for their last meal before sleeping the day away in some nearby cave.

I lowered my glasses and focused on the cantinas. A drunk staggered out of an alley and collapsed in front of the La Rosa, the cantina on my right. He looked familiar. I screwed the eyepieces around to get a closer look at him and was surprised to see a familiar face. Wondering what the hell the tall young cowboy was doing down here, I checked the other cantina, La Perla. The smaller of the two, it was located near the crumbling missionary walls. It was also on the other side of the main street, which wasn't really a street but merely a continuation of the original cattle trail. After cutting through the village it crossed a small stretch of desert and then started its long and arduous climb up to the foothills below the *Sierra Madre Occidental*.

Disappointed that I hadn't seen any sign of the Guthrie brothers, I tucked the glasses back into my saddlebag, mounted and rode into the village. There was a small rundown livery stable a few doors down from the La Rosa. An old white-haired Mexican, with fine drooping mustaches, was taking a siesta against one wall. He was snoring softly and had such a contented look on his lined, leathery brown face I didn't have the heart to wake him. But I needed to know if the Guthries' horses were in the stables, so dismounting I walked quietly to the large, sagging door. It wasn't locked and I was about to drag it open when I heard a dull click behind me. I knew the sound well and slowly raised my hands.

'No need to shoot, old man,' I said

without turning. 'I'm not going to steal anything.'

'It is good that you are not, *señor*,' the old Mexican replied. 'It is considered poor manners to kill *gringos* before breakfast.'

'I am glad you are such a civilized man,' I said wryly. 'Okay if I turn around?'

'*Si, señor*. But it would be wise not to lower your hands.'

Keeping my hands up, I turned around and found myself looking down the barrel of an old single shot, percussion lock dueling pistol that was so rusted, I doubted it would fire.

Not wanting to insult the old Mexican, who was now standing, I managed not to smile. 'Is this your stable?' I asked him politely.

'*Si, señor*. And my father's before me and before that his father's also. Now,' he added, 'I have answered enough of your questions, *gringo*. Give me your name, *por favor*, and tell me what your business is here.'

'Name's Lute Latimore, *señor*. I'm looking for three men, outlaws, who are wanted for murder in my country.'

'You expect to find them in my stable?'

'No. But it's possible their horses are in there.'

The old Mexican mulled over my words before saying: 'And if they are, *señor*? What then?'

'That means they're hiding in San Cristobal somewhere. I have business with them.'

The old Mexican's smile turned his leathery brown face into a mass of wrinkles. 'I am glad to hear that, *señor*. When I am next at prayer, I will offer ten Hail Marys for you.'

'Does that mean I can open the door?'

'Open it as you wish, *señor*. But there is no need. The horses you look for are in there. I stabled them myself yesterday while the sun was still high.'

'What about the men — any idea where I might find them?'

'*Si, señor.*' The old Mexican tucked the ancient dueling pistol into his sash. 'I will lead you to them.'

'*Gracias.*'

'*Por nada.*'

I couldn't resist adding: 'Aren't you afraid that old piece might go off and leave you missing a few parts?'

The old Mexican looked at me with a mischievous twinkle in his dark brown eyes. 'At my age, *señor*, there are no parts left to miss.'

# 15

I accompanied the old Mexican, who said his name was Eduardo Hierra, back to the main street. Dawn had brightened into early morning. The sun was in my eyes and I pulled my hat brim down so I didn't have to squint.

The first thing I noticed was that the tall young cowboy was no longer passed out in front of the La Rosa. I wondered where he was and wished I had time to look for him and take him back across the border with me. But finding the Guthrie brothers was all that mattered right now, so I followed the old Mexican across the street to the La Perla.

The swing-doors were closed but I could hear mariachi music playing inside. Suddenly two shots were fired. Women screamed. Raucous drunken laughter followed. Then a girl screamed and almost immediately two men began arguing. I recognized their voices. They belonged to Bryce and Gibby Guthrie.

Instantly I thought of Heck and rage burned through me. I signaled to the old Mexican to stay back. Then, Colt in hand, I kicked open the cantina door and stepped inside.

The three brothers were sitting in the corner, tequila bottles and glasses on the table before them, each embracing a whore on his lap. The girls' dresses were open in front, revealing their ample breasts, and the brothers were pouring tequila over them and then licking it off to everyone's delight.

Slumped over the table next to them was the tall young cowboy. He had passed out. In one hand he clutched his ever-present tequila bottle, while the other hung limply beside his holstered six-shooter, a long-barreled .44. The gun and the holster surprised me. The bottom of the holster was cut off and the gun-sight had been filed down. It was the kind of fast-draw rig used by gunfighters, not cowboys, and I wondered what the hell he was doing with it. But he'd seemed so damned harmless and was always so damned drunk I figured he was living some kind of gunslinger fantasy and shrugged it off.

Besides, I had the Guthries to deal with. They looked up as I entered, startled to see me.

'Let me see a show of hands,' I barked.

Seeing my Colt aimed at them, they sullenly obeyed.

I jerked my thumb at the whores, adding: '*Vamos! Vamos!*'

Alarmed, the whores scrambled off the brothers' laps and fled.

'Okay,' I told the Guthries. 'On your feet!'

Then, when they didn't move:

'Do it! *Pronto!*' I fired a shot that nicked Gibby's uninjured ear.

He yelped and grabbed it, cursing me.

'Or maybe you'd sooner lose both

ears?' I fired again, nicking his other ear and reopening the old injury.

Gibby squealed, grabbed his bleeding ear and jumped up. His brothers also got to their feet, glaring at me, hands drifting toward their six-guns.

'That's close enough,' I warned. 'Or my next bullet buys you an unmarked grave!'

Doke, whose wounded arm was in a makeshift sling, and Bryce sullenly moved their hands away from their guns.

Behind them the tall young cowboy stirred in his sleep. My shots had awakened him and suddenly he sat up, groggily looked around, gave a stupid grin and then fell face-down on the table.

'You,' I said, signaling to a whore standing between two half-drunk cowboys at the bar. 'Get over here.'

Frightened, she timidly approached me. 'I cause no trouble, *señor*,' she pleaded. 'You no hurt me, *por favor*.'

'Do as I say and *nobody'll* get hurt,' I promised.

'What you want me to do, señor?'

I thumbed at the brothers. 'Get their guns, one by one, and throw them in the corner over there.' I indicated the floor behind the young cowboy.

Wide-eyed with fear, the whore went to Doke and reached for his six-gun.

'Easy,' I warned her. 'Go nice and slow. And you,' I told Doke, 'you keep grabbing air else I'll do what I'd really like to do, and that's shoot you full of holes.'

Doke didn't move. Keeping his good hand raised, he glared at me with such hatred I was tempted to shoot him so he could never get the jump on me.

The whore tossed his gun on the floor and then moved over in front of Gibby. Slowly removing his gun, she threw it after the other. She then pulled Bryce's Colt from its holster and tossed it away. It slithered across the floor and slammed against a brass spittoon, causing a loud clanging sound.

Instantly the tall young cowboy sat up, startled, and looked around.

'Wha' the hell?' he exclaimed.

'Go back to sleep,' I told him.

If he heard me, he didn't show it.

'You got trouble with these fellas, marshal?' he said, referring to the Guthrie brothers.

'What's between me and them,' I replied, 'is none of your damn business.' I thumbed back the hammer of my Colt. 'So either go the hell back to sleep or take a walk.'

He studied me for another moment, yawned, stretched and stood up. 'Be seeing you, marshal.' He strode to the door, his step surprisingly steady for a man who appeared to be drunk. There, he looked back at me, yawned again and said: 'If you change your mind and need me for anything, look me up. I'm at the hotel.' He pushed out through the bat-wing doors.

I turned back to Doke, Gibby and Bryce.

'Unbuckle your gun-belts and put 'em on the table. Do it,' I said as they hesitated. 'All I need is the slightest reason to shoot you. All of you!'

Grudgingly, they obeyed.

'Now the belts holding up your pants. C'mon,' I barked as again they hesitated. 'Get 'em off.'

I waited until each brother had removed his belt. 'Okay,' I said to Bryce. 'Now tie Gibby's hands behind his back.'

When he'd finished, I told Bryce to tie Doke's hands in front of him with one of the other belts.

'Now, all of you turn around,' I said when he'd finished. When he obeyed, I stuck out my free hand for the last belt. Bryce deliberately dropped it. I told him to kick it over to me. He did. I fastened his hands behind his back and ordered the three of them to start walking.

'Where to?' Doke growled.

'Out the door would be a good start. Then to the stables.'

'You're never going to get us back across the border,' Bryce said.

'Maybe not,' I said. 'But I'm sure

going to enjoy shooting you if I don't.' I prodded him in the back with my Colt. 'Now get moving.'

# 16

Keeping a step behind the brothers I marched them across the street to the livery stables. There I tossed the hostler some pesos and told him to saddle our horses. I then untied the Guthrie's hands and covered them with my Colt.

The brothers didn't say a word. But they all kept looking quizzically at me as if trying to figure out why I was so anxious to take them back to the U.S., where they would either rot in prison or hang.

Finally Doke growled at me: 'Why you got this hard-on for us, marshal? We never done you no harm.'

'Hell,' added Bryce, 'you ain't still holding a grudge against us for shooting up that hotel some years back, are you?'

'Marshall Heck already locked us up for that,' Gibby chimed in.

'Yeah, and on top of that we paid the money the judge fined us,' reminded Bryce. 'I'd say we was even on that score.'

'This has nothing to do with that hotel,' I said grimly.

'What then?' demanded Doke.

'Don't press your luck,' I warned. 'You know damned well why I'm rousting you.'

'Tell us anyway,' Doke said. ''Case we was drunk before.'

Fighting down the desire to shoot him, I said: 'One or all of you killed my brother, Heck.'

The three brothers reacted as if they were genuinely surprised.

'What the hell you talking 'bout?' Gibby said.

'Heck Latimore, Deputy U.S. Marshal of Canyon Diablo. You gunned him down outside the Texas Saloon.'

Again, the brothers exchanged puzzled looks before turning back to me.

'That's crazy talk,' Doke said. 'We never even saw your brother that night.'

'Damned straight,' said Gibby. 'And even if we had, we wasn't in no condition to shoot him.'

'He's right,' added Doke. 'After we was all done playing poker, we got so skunked we had to sleep it off upstairs in one of the whore's bedrooms.'

'Can ask anyone,' insisted Bryce. 'Bartender, the whores — anyone.'

'Whoever said we killed your brother, marshal,' Gibby said, 'is a goddamn liar!'

'Or just plain mistaken,' added Doke.

They sounded convincing, but I wasn't fooled.

'You're wasting your breath,' I said. 'Some folks saw the three of you riding away after you killed Heck. And 'fore you deny it, they recognized your pinto,' I said to Bryce.

'I ain't the only one who rides a pinto,' he protested. 'Hap Rogers over to the Slant-Bar-G has two of 'em, a mare and a — '

I cut him off. 'Save your damn lies! Someone also heard you talking at the bar, saying how after you took care of my brother you were heading for the border.'

'That was me,' admitted Doke. 'But I never said it like that. What I said was, 'after we cash ourselves in, then we'll take care of your brother.''

'We owed him money from a game of five card stud the night before,' began Gibby.

I stopped him. 'More goddamn lies! My brother never played poker or any other card game. Said gambling offended God.'

Gibby made a scoffing sound. 'Who you kidding, marshal?'

'He might've told you that,' Doke said, ''cause he didn't want you to know. But he was lying through his teeth, 'cause he sure as hell played. He was mighty partial to craps, too.'

I'd heard enough. Flaring, I bounced my Colt off Doke's head. He dropped without a sound and lay crumpled at my feet.

Bryce quickly knelt beside his older

brother, cradled Doke's head on his knees and glared at me. 'You had no call to do that, marshal.'

'Maybe next time he'll think twice 'fore calling my brother a liar,' I said. 'Now, get him on his feet and onto his horse. And you two do the same, or I swear I'll gun you down right where you stand.'

Eyes full of hatred, Gibby and Bryce helped their brother up. He was conscious but wobbly-legged and would have fallen but for their support. I stepped back and kept my gun trained on them as they helped Doke onto his horse and then mounted themselves.

I then swung up onto my horse and wagged my Colt at them. 'Move out.'

Leaving the stables, we rode in single file down the main street in the direction of the border. On both sides of us curious white-clad villagers, their brown faces hidden beneath tall-crowned, wide-brimmed sombreros, watched as we rode past.

I didn't expect any trouble from

them. But just in case some of them were friends of the Guthrie brothers I kept my hand on the butt of my Colt, ready to draw and shoot at the slightest interference.

It was then the mongrels rushed up. Half-starved, they ran alongside us, barking and nipping at the heels of the horses. They didn't seem to bother the brothers' horses, but they drove the mare crazy. I could barely control her as she kept lunging at them, trying to bite them. And when they easily avoided her teeth, she tried to kick them. I shouted at them, and when that didn't drive them away I shot one of them. My bullet creased its bony haunches and it ran off yelping. It must have been the leader, because almost immediately the rest of the pack followed it.

Relieved, I holstered my Colt and tried to bring the feisty little mare under control. It took a few moments, but gradually I felt her settling down under me and was able to return my full attention to the Guthrie brothers.

Ahead, the street narrowed as it neared the outskirts of the little village. This brought the rundown shacks on both sides in much closer. Worried that the brothers might try to take advantage of this and spur their horses between the shacks, I pulled my Winchester from its boot, levered in a round and rested the rifle across my saddle horn.

Bryce, who was closest to me, looked back and grinned. 'What's the matter, marshal? 'Fraid we'll make a break for it?'

'Not afraid,' I said, 'hoping. See, if you take off, or even *look* like you're going to make a break for it, then shooting you won't bother my conscience in the leas — ' I broke off, startled, as a woman emerged from one of the shacks carrying a basin of soapy water. Not expecting anyone to be passing, she threw the dishwater into the street.

Most of it splashed over the mare's head. Panicking, Chloe reared up, snorting and pawing at the air with her forelegs, throwing me off her back.

I landed hard and lay there in the dirt, stunned. When I came around and could see again, Doke had dismounted and was standing over me. I tried to sit up but he kicked me in the face. I went sprawling, pinpoints of light exploding before my eyes. Everything slowly faded into the distance.

The last sound I heard before blacking out was a distant rifle shot.

# 17

When I regained consciousness, I was sitting in an old hard-backed chair outside the shack, and the same woman who'd tossed the water was now bathing my forehead with a wet towel. She was rambling on in Spanish, most of which I didn't understand, and kept turning and brandishing her hands in dismay at someone standing nearby.

I blinked away the last of the cobwebs and realized it was the tall young cowboy.

'How you feeling, fella?' he drawled as my eyes opened. 'That was one hell of a kick he planted on you.'

I wanted to answer him but the words wouldn't come. My head was threatening to pound off my shoulders and my right cheek and jaw were so swollen and stiff, I could barely open my mouth. I gingerly glanced about me, looking for the Guthrie brothers.

'Don't worry 'bout them, partner,' the tall young cowboy said, 'they skedaddled soon as I began shooting at them. Here,' he added, holding an earthen cup to my mouth, 'drink this. It'll help deaden the pain.'

I managed to crack open my lips wide enough to swallow the tequila. I could see clearly now and took a long look at my rescuer. He seemed even taller, lankier and more boyish-looking close up. He had pale blue eyes in a lean tanned face and a mess of white-blond hair that refused to stay in place no matter how many times he combed it back with his long slender fingers. The now-familiar bottle of tequila still poked out of the pocket of his jacket but his eyes were clear and when he spoke, his speech wasn't slurred by alcohol. In fact, he seemed cold sober.

'Too bad they got away,' he went on, 'I was hoping you'd do my job for me.'

'Y-Y-Your job?' I croaked.

'Yep.' He took a wallet from an inner

pocket, flipped it open to show a Texas Ranger badge and ID inside. 'I've been after the Guthries for nigh on two months now. Finally tailed them down here, where of course I got no jurisdiction so I couldn't arrest them, and then, here you come, rounding them up and taking them back 'cross the border nice as you please — ' He broke off to answer something the woman had asked. Whatever he said seemed to satisfy her because she stopped bathing my forehead and went into the shack.

'She feels mighty bad for what she done,' the tall young cowboy explained. 'I told her it wasn't her fault, just the luck of the draw, but, hell, she don't see it that way and — '

'Who are you?' I said, cutting him off.

'I just showed you, partner. J.P. Rascomb, Texas Ranger.'

My eyes strayed to the bottle in his pocket. He must have noticed because suddenly he laughed, bent over and slapped his skinny thighs.

'You're wondering how if I'm a Texas Ranger, like I claim, I'm full as a tick most of the time.'

'It did cross my mind,' I admitted.

J.P. Rascomb pulled the bottle from his pocket and held it to my lips. 'No, no, go ahead,' he insisted when I pulled back. 'Take a swig. I guarantee you'll like it.'

I reluctantly took a sip and realized it was only water.

'Finest branch water in the whole state of Texas,' J.P. said proudly. 'I ought to know. Comes straight from a creek runs right through my daddy's property. Wherever I go I always bring a bunch of bottles of it with me.'

I eyed him with new-found respect. 'You make one hell of a drunk,' I said.

'Had good teachers. My daddy, uncles, even most of my cousins, they all learned real young how to bend an elbow. Me, now, I never became partial to liquor. But it makes for good cover and I figured it was the only way I could keep an eye on the Guthries without them getting suspicious.'

'Sure had me fooled,' I admitted, adding: 'You could've told me, you know? After all, we are both lawmen and out of professional courtesy — '

'I know, I know,' J.P. said. 'And I intended to but' — he grinned mischievously — 'I just wanted to see how long I could fool you.'

'Well, you sure did that,' I said, thinking, one day my turn would come. Then, 'How long was I out?' I asked.

'Not long. But soon as you're up to it, Hoss, we ought to make dust 'fore them gunnies get too big a jump on us.'

'Then let's not waste another second.' I extended my hand and he helped me up. For a few seconds the world spun crazily around me.

'Whoa, whoa,' J.P. said, grabbing my arm. 'Maybe we should give you a few more minutes.'

I shook my head. 'Just get me on my horse, J.P. Let me worry 'bout hanging on.'

# 18

Talking was damned painful for me so we rode in silence back across the border. J.P. was blessed with keen eyesight and consequently we were able to follow the Guthrie brothers' tracks a lot easier and at a much faster pace. That pleased the mare and she wasn't as skittish as she had been on the ride down.

Once we were back in Arizona, the brothers' tracks led us northeast in the direction of Tombstone and Cochise's former stronghold, the Dragoon Mountains. We'd been riding at a steady clip and we reined up to give the horses a breather.

'Doesn't make sense,' I said, sipping warm, metallic-tasting water from my canteen. 'Even though Cochise is dead the territory is still crawling with Apaches.'

J.P. frowned, puzzled. 'Where else would you go if you had stolen rifles to sell?'

'The Guthries are selling guns to the Chiricahuas?'

'Chiricahuas, White Mountain, Tontos, Jicarilla — you name the tribe, the brothers are selling to them. You didn't know?' he added, seeing my surprise. 'Hell's fire, partner, they got themselves a real sweet setup going on. Their cousin, Cory, is the supply master for several of the forts in Arizona. He orders the rifles for the troops and then notifies the Guthries when the supply train will be arriving. They rob it 'fore it reaches the fort, sell the guns to the Apaches and split the profits with their cousin. Hell, the whole operation couldn't run more smoothly if the army itself had sanctioned it.'

'If you know all this,' I said, 'why haven't you done something about it?'

'Knowing it and proving it is horses of different colors, partner. But I'm getting closer all the time. And when I do get the goods on them, believe me I'll really enjoy watching the bastards swing!' He paused, gave me a concerned look, said: 'I know you got a more personal stake in this, losing your brother and all. But I got family myself in the cavalry and the thought of them being gunned down by carbines sold to Apaches by dirt-grubbing polecats like the Guthries — well, it fair gets my blood to boiling!'

I felt the same way and it gave me an idea. 'Tell you what, J.P. Let's you and me agree on something.'

'Name it.'

'Let's swear to track down these no-good sonsofbitches and kill them — not arrest 'em — *kill* them, even if it takes us the rest of our goddamn lives!'

'Partner,' J.P. drawled, 'you took the words right out of my mouth. Put it there.' He offered me his hand and I shook it firmly.

# 19

I've known it to get plenty hot during my years in Arizona and New Mexico, but I swear it was never hotter than it was during our ride to Tombstone. The sun blazed down on us with an oppressive relentlessness that seemed almost devilish in its desire to turn us into burnt toast. The heat also took its toll on our horses and we couldn't push them as hard as we wanted for fear of killing them. As a result, it was late afternoon by the time we rode into Tombstone. By then we were caked with sweat and close to melting.

I hadn't been to Tombstone in some time. In fact the last time I was there was shortly after the town's first U.S. Marshal, Fred White, was accidentally shot and killed by one of Ike Clanton's clan, a loud-mouthed braggart named

Curly Bill Brocius. Just about every-body has their own version of what happened and most of them have a grain of truth in them. But from what Wyatt Earp told me, Curly Bill was drunkenly shooting in the air when Marshal White confronted him and insisted he hand over his gun. Curly Bill started to obey him and then changed his mind. White tried to grab it from him and during the ensuing tug-of-war, the gun went off and the marshal was shot in the groin. At first it hadn't appeared to be a fatal wound, but complications arose during the night and White died two days later. White was well-liked and the citizens wanted to lynch Curly Bill, so Wyatt, who was the Deputy Marshal, spirited him out of town and kept him locked up in Tucson until it was time for his trial. I didn't attend the trial, but I do know that Curly Bill was acquitted. All he had to do was serve a few days in jail for involuntary manslaughter and pay a fine for drunkenly discharging a weapon in a public place, but after that he was released.

The townspeople were outraged. They claimed that Ike Clanton had bribed the judge and intimidated the jury so that Curly Bill could go free. But Wyatt swore it wasn't true. He said it was not only common knowledge that Brocius and White were friends, but before his death White had given a sworn affidavit exonerating Curly Bill, saying that the gun had fired accidentally.

Personally I don't like Curly Bill. He's a rustler, a gunman and a known troublemaker. But even I had to admit that he seemed genuinely broken up about killing his friend.

After White died, Wyatt Earp and his brothers took over as town marshals and with the help of an ill-tempered, trigger-happy dentist named John Henry Holliday prodded Ike Clanton and his gang into a gunfight in an alley near the O.K. Corral on East Allen Street. Predictably, the Earps and

Holliday won the day. Since then much has been made of the shootout with some folks who weren't even there glorifying it, others exaggerating the number of deaths and how long it lasted. But according to Wyatt, the shootout only lasted thirty seconds and when it was over Virgil and Holliday had been wounded, and three of the Clanton gang were killed while the others were chased into hiding.

I'd known Doc, as Holliday was called, ever since he'd arrived in Tombstone. He wasn't a pleasant man and I didn't like him much, but tried to overlook his irascibility because I knew he was a lunger with one foot in the grave. I also knew the woman he'd taken up with, a smart, fun-loving whore named Mary Cummings, or Big Nose Kate. Everybody liked Kate, including me, and I promised myself that after J.P. and I had dealt with the Guthries, I'd drag her away from Doc long enough for us to have dinner together in the plush, recently-built Grand Hotel.

Now, as the two of us rode past the Crystal Palace, a large ornate building on the corner of 5$^{th}$ and Allen Streets, J.P. interrupted my thoughts by suggesting we stable the horses and search for the Guthrie brothers on foot. First though, he insisted we have a beer and then track down Wyatt and ask him if he'd seen the Guthries or knew where they were hiding out. 'Truthfully, I hate to get the S.O.B. involved,' J.P. added, ''cause, sure as holy hell he'll want to be in charge and then take all the credit when we run the Guthries to ground. But on the other hand, if he can lead us to the Guthries, I reckon we'd be damned fools not to seek his help.'

'Say no more,' I said, wiping the sweat from my eyes. 'As far as I'm concerned, Wyatt can take all the goddamn credit in the world, and then some. It don't matter two licks to me. Way I feel right now, Jesus, I'd shake hands with the Devil himself if I thought he'd lead us to the Guthries.'

'And I'd be right behind you,' J.P.

said, wiping his brow. 'Man alive, Hades must be on fire for it to be this damned hot.'

We were approaching The Bird Cage Theater and suddenly I couldn't make myself go any farther without first drowning my thirst.

'Beer's on me,' I said. And before J.P. could argue, I reined in and gently nudged the weary mare up to the hitch-rail.

J.P. dismounted and tied up alongside me. His shirt was black with sweat and sticking to his body. He looked drained and weary. But he managed to grin and said: 'You may not know it, Hoss, but you just saved my life.'

Before going inside, we dunked our hats into the rain-barrel at the side of the square, adobe-brick building and held them under the mouths of our thirsty horses. They drank greedily and would have gladly drank more if we'd let them. But not wanting them to bloat up, we loosened their cinches and then went inside for a drink.

The Bird Cage wasn't just a theater with voluptuous, painted dancing girls. For those who weren't satisfied with watching the stage-show or quenching their thirst at the saloon bar, there was a basement gambling parlor where sometimes Doc Holliday dealt faro, and fourteen 'cages' or theater boxes that ran along both sides of the main hall, facing the stage. Each cage seated four and had its own prostitutes, who discreetly closed the long red drapes whenever they entertained their customers.

I'd been 'entertained' myself there a few times. I'd also lost many a week's wages in the poker parlor. But like most of the regular customers, I always enjoyed myself and never regretted a dollar or a moment spent in The Bird Cage!

Now, as J.P. and I walked into the main hall the orchestra was warming up prior to the next show. The raucous crowd drinking at the tables facing the stage was made up mostly of miners, prospectors and cowhands that hadn't been to town or seen a woman in months. Bearded and unwashed and smelling worse than hog slop, they were eager to spend their hard-earned gold dust or nuggets to get liquored up and to holler at the heavily-rouged, scantily-clad dancers. Most of the girls were young, eager to please and worth looking at. But a few were long in the tooth. To make up for it, they wore their short frilly skirts as high as possible and kicked their silk-stocking-legs even higher in an effort to encourage the howling audience to pelt them with nuggets and coins.

J.P. and I stopped just inside the entrance and after making sure the Guthrie brothers weren't part of the audience, took a long hard look at the men sitting in the boxes. But our luck had turned sour. None of them were Guthries.

'Let's grab that beer and then go find Wyatt,' I said to J.P.

'Good idea,' he replied. 'But let's not

linger too long. A fella could get distracted from his duty real easy here.'

'Or even end up chasing the rabbit,' I said, grinning.

'Hoss, you're reading my mind.' J.P. laughed like a schoolboy caught with his pants down.

The long highly-polished wooden bar stood against one wall in the saloon and since the chorus girls weren't on-stage yet, most of them were earning extra tips by mingling with the mob of drunken miners and prospectors. The others were entertaining the local businessmen and sunburned eastern drummers in their trail-soiled suits, bowties and starched white collars stiff enough to cut their throats.

Elbowing our way up to the bar we ordered two beers from a sweating, red-faced barkeep whose bulging muscles, pushed-in nose and cauli-flower ears indicated he'd once been a prize fighter. But fisticuffs weren't what he was famous for. His pride and joy was his magnificent handlebar mustache. Chestnut red, it stretched from cheek to cheek with both ends heavily waxed and curled upward into sharp points. As he left to draw our beers, J.P. shook his head enviously.

'I'd give a year's wages to be able to grow a mustache like that,' he grumbled.

'So, what's stopping you? Jesus, with your color hair, it'd catch the eye of every gal from here to Phoenix.'

J.P. waited until the barkeep set our beers before us and then hurried off to serve another customer before saying glumly: 'It ain't the color that's the problem, Hoss.'

'What, then?'

'It's the hair itself.'

'Meaning?'

'The hair on my upper lip is so fine, no matter how long I grow it, it never gets thick enough to make any kind of mustache, let alone a beauty like that barkeep's!' As he spoke J.P. looked at his reflection in the large wood-framed mirror behind the bar, his fingers proudly curling the ends of an imaginary handlebar mustache. Then he caught me grinning at him and jerked his hands away, embarrassed, grabbed his beer, blew the froth off the top and drank half of it in one long gulp.

Chuckling, I drank some of my own beer, thinking as I did that nothing compared to a tall cool Falstaff when you were hot and thirsty. As I set my glass down and wiped the froth from my lips, I glimpsed a familiar face among all the other faces reflected in the back-bar mirror.

'Talking of handlebar mustaches,' I said, indicating the customers behind us, 'there's one to envy.'

J.P. turned and saw Wyatt Earp talking to a tall gaunt man with a sallow complexion who from the cut of his clothes could have been a gambler, a well-dressed businessman, or maybe even an easterner.

'Damn him,' J.P. growled as he stared enviously at Earp's huge mustache that seemed even larger when compared to his slender, high-cheekboned face. 'Why the hell does *he* deserve to grow a mustache like that and I don't?'

'Let's go ask him,' I said, finishing my beer. 'You know Wyatt. Man's never lost for an answer.'

By the time we'd elbowed our way up to Wyatt, he'd seen us coming and gestured for us to meet him outside.

'Sonofabitch must have some under-the-table shenanigans going on with Holliday,' J.P. said as we changed directions and pushed through the crowd toward the entrance. 'He's afraid if Doc sees us hanging around, it'll queer the deal.'

Surprised by the venom in J.P.'s normally easygoing voice, I said: 'Remind me never to grow a handlebar mustache if that's how you're going to talk 'bout me.'

'You go to hell,' J.P. said. But he was grinning as he said it.

As we reached the front door, we heard the orchestra start playing the overture in the theater. Immediately, loud cheering and catcalling followed and moments later here came the chorus girls singing 'When Johnny comes marching home again, hurrah, hurrah!'

'I hate that damn song,' J.P. said.

'Why?' I asked, surprised. 'I would've thought that you, from Johnny Reb country yourself, couldn't hear enough of it.'

J.P. didn't answer right away. But his scowl couldn't hide the pain he was feeling.

'Look,' I said, realizing I'd struck a nerve, 'I was just funning you, *amigo*. So let's drop the subject and — '

'It's my daddy,' J.P. blurted.

'What about him?'

'Whenever I hear this song it makes me think of him.'

'Why? Was his name Johnny?'

'Yeah,' J.P. said bitterly. 'But he never came marching home from the goddamn war!'

'Jesus, I'm sorry. I didn't know.'

'It's okay,' J.P. said. 'Reckon I'm over it now.'

I sensed he was anything but over it. Feeling bad for bringing it up, I followed him outside. The sun was going down but it was still stiflingly hot. We stood there for a few minutes by a sign marked: East Allen Street, and then Wyatt finally came out and joined us. At first he didn't speak or even look at us. He warily watched the pedestrians and riders moving past us as if to make sure that none of them were a threat to him. Then, satisfied he wasn't in any jeopardy he turned and offered me his hand.

'Lute . . . '

'Wyatt.'

'What brings you to Tombstone?'

'We're after the Guthrie brothers,' I said, adding: 'You know J.P., I reckon?'

Wyatt nodded, hard-eyed, but offered no greeting. At best, he wasn't a friendly man. Now, as he and J.P. stared at each other and made no attempt to shake hands, I sensed real friction between them and wondered what their history was.

'What do you want the Guthries for?' Wyatt asked, turning back to me.

'They gunned down my brother.'

Wyatt showed honest emotion for the first time. 'Heck's *dead*?' he said, shocked and dismayed. 'Christ-on-a-cross! When?'

'Week ago in Canyon Diablo.'

'Damn!' He was briefly silent as he digested the news. 'I'm powerful sorry, Lute,' he said then. 'I liked your brother. Heck was a good man and a damned fine marshal.' He absently stroked his mustache. 'I didn't figure the Guthries for that kind of sand.'

'Doesn't take much sand to shoot a man in the back,' I said grimly.

Wyatt looked disgusted. 'Figures! I never did trust that bunch of vermin.'

'Have you got any idea where they are or — '

'I don't, Lute. Only wish to hell I did. 'Bout all I know is they've left town.'

'How long since you last saw them?' J.P. asked.

'I never *did* see them,' Wyatt said. 'Jim did.'

'Your older brother?'

Wyatt nodded. 'He came busting into the office 'bout two hours ago saying he'd just seen them riding away from the Crystal Palace.'

'Maybe we should talk to him,' J.P. said to me.

'He's not here,' Wyatt said. 'James had to ride over to Ma Strickland's place, to talk to her 'bout some stolen horses. He'll be back some time tonight, though.'

I had an idea. 'Would it be okay with you, Wyatt, if J.P. and I question the workers at the Crystal Palace? You know, in case one of them happened to hear where the Guthries were headed.'

'Better yet,' Wyatt said, 'I'll go with you to make sure you get some answers.' He turned before either I or J.P. could argue and strode off toward the Crystal Palace.

J.P. shot me a sour look. 'Easy to see why everyone calls him Mr. Likable.'

'Let me handle him,' I said as we hurried after Wyatt. 'For some reason he's always treated me like family.'

# 20

The Crystal Palace had recently been burned down by a fire that swept through it. I wasn't in Tombstone at the time but from all accounts the townspeople had rallied and the building was quickly rebuilt, this time with an additional second floor made up of offices. From what Wyatt told me, his brother Virgil, then a Deputy U.S. Marshal, had occupied one of the offices. But after the O.K. Corral gunfight, when he was severely wounded by ambushers, he'd left Tombstone and taken his family to California to recuperate.

Virg and I had been good friends. He was a fine lawman with great integrity and I admired him far more than I did Wyatt, who frankly was more interested in gambling than upholding the law, and I missed not having Virg around.

Now, as Wyatt, J.P. and I entered the

Crystal Palace, I saw it was full of customers that Wyatt derisively called 'freeloaders' or 'peanut boozers' — men who arrived early to devour the bowls of peanuts and pretzels put out on the bar as an enticement to get them to drink. They felt they were getting the best of the deal and often joked about getting a 'free meal' with their beer. But what they didn't realize was that the bartenders sprinkled additional salt on the peanuts and pretzels, knowing it would make everyone extra thirsty. As a result the freeloaders ended up drinking far more beer than they had intended, and never knew why.

The sight of three lawmen — especially Wyatt's grim, tight-lipped presence — deflated some of the crowd's rowdy enthusiasm. But once they knew why we were there, they relaxed and willingly answered our questions.

It was the same with the employees. They were cooperative. But like the customers, they couldn't help us. Most of them had seen the Guthrie brothers drinking at the bar, and some of them saw the brothers leave. But none of them had any idea where the Guthries went after leaving the saloon.

Disappointed, the three of us had a beer at the bar and then left. It was getting dark outside and Wyatt, who had his finger in almost every saloon, gambling parlor and brothel, suggested we spend the night at one of his rooming houses rather than roughing it under the stars.

Before J.P. or I could decide, a wiry old prospector named Flapjack Hamlet sidled up to us. No bigger than a ten-year-old, his clothes were ragged and filthy and he smelled worse than a dead goat. But he was eager to talk to us and after making sure no one was watching, said for the price of a drink he'd tell us where the Guthrie brothers were headed.

I dug out a silver dollar, intending to give it to the scrawny old man, but Wyatt stopped me. 'Withholding information,' he warned Flapjack, 'is a criminal offense. So if you know anything about the Guthries, you old fart, you better spill your guts or I'll lock your deadbeat ass up for the night!'

Flapjack knew better than argue with Wyatt. And after whining about being treated unfairly, he said: 'Saw 'em. Did indeed. Yep. They was digging. Dug up something. I saw 'em. Did indeed. Digging and digging, like they was grave-robbers.'

'Where?' I said. 'Where were they digging?'

Flapjack removed his filthy campaign hat and scratched his bald head in an effort to remember. When nothing came, he briefly picked his nose, screwed up his weathered, sunken-cheeked face and hopped from one foot to the other a few times. Still nothing came to him.

'Dammit, man,' Wyatt exclaimed angrily, 'think!'

'Am,' Flapjack said. He picked his nose again and did a few more hops. 'Trying.'

'Well, try harder,' barked Wyatt.

'Trying harder,' Flapjack repeated. His hopping grew more frantic.

Feeling sorry for him, I said: 'Was it far from here?'

Flapjack shook his head and picked at his toothless gums with a dirty thumbnail.

'Nearby?' J.P. said.

'Show you,' the grizzled old prospector said. 'Follow ol' Flapjack.'

He led us around in back of the Crystal Palace. There, within spitting distance of the rear entrance, was a freshly dug hole in the ground about the size of a grave.

'Did you see what they dug up?' I asked Flapjack.

He nodded eagerly and held up two wrinkled fingers.

'Two what?' J.P. said. 'Bodies?'

Flapjack shook his head and continued to hold up his two wrinkled fingers.

'What then?' Wyatt demanded.

'Coffins, looked like.'

'Coffins?' I said. 'You sure, old timer?'

''Cept they weren't,' Flapjack said.

'Weren't what?' J.P. asked.

'Coffins.'

'But you just said — '

'Boxes,' said Flapjack. 'More like. It's true. Yep. Saw 'em. Did indeed.'

'C'mon, you two,' Wyatt said impatiently. 'We're wasting our time here.'

'No, no, wait,' I said. Then to Flapjack: 'Boxes that looked like coffins — is that what you saw being dug up?'

'Yep. That's it! Boxes like coffins being dug up. 'Cept they weren't.'

'What the hell were they then?' Wyatt said, frustrated.

'Boxes like coffins,' repeated Flapjack. He hopped around, agitated, his frail voice cracking with emotion as he said: 'That's what Flapjack saw all right. Yes I did. Did indeed. Can believe me or not. That's what I saw.'

'We believe you. We really do,' J.P. said, adding: 'And these boxes like coffins you saw — did you happen to see what was in them?'

Flapjack shook his head. 'Couldn't.

Wasn't open. No, sir. All closed tight. But I saw 'em all right. Yep. Sure did. Did indeed.'

I tuned him out as he rambled on and tried to visualize what he saw or thought he saw in his almost delusional state. For a moment nothing happened. Then it suddenly hit me.

'Rifles!' I exclaimed.

J.P. and Wyatt turned to me, frowning.

'What about them?' J.P. said.

'That's what was in the boxes!'

'Rifles?'

'Sure.'

'Why rifles?' Wyatt said.

''Cause that's where the Guthries hid the last shipment they got when they robbed the army supply train.'

'Not rifles,' Flapjack said eagerly. 'Coffins. Wooden boxes.'

'Yeah, yeah, boxes,' I said, slipping him the silver dollar. 'Now I need you to do something for me — I want you to concentrate.'

'Concentrate,' Flapjack repeated. 'Can

do that. Yep. Indeed I can.'

'Good. Now here's what I want you to concentrate on. After the men dug up the boxes, can you remember which way they went?'

'Yep. Flapjack remembers all right. Yep. Do indeed.'

'And which way was that?'

Flapjack grinned, showing toothless, tobacco-stained gums, and pointed toward the Dragoon Mountains.

'The mountains?' I said. 'Is that what you're pointing at?'

Flapjack nodded and beamed, pleased with himself. 'Dragoons,' he said proudly.

'You absolutely sure about that?' I pressed.

He nodded again. 'Once Flapjack find gold there. Many years ago. Yep. You go?'

'You bet,' I said. I patted him on his thin bony shoulder. 'Thanks, old timer. You've been a great help.'

'You want Flapjack to take you there? Find more gold?' He looked eagerly at us.

'No, thanks,' J.P. said. 'We'll take it from here.'

Flapjack scurried off before Wyatt could stop him.

'Crazy old coot,' he said. 'Can't believe a goddamn thing he says.'

'I believe him,' I said.

'So do I,' added J.P.

Wyatt shrugged. 'Fine. Suit yourselves. But you fellas better wait till morning before you leave. Then I'll round up some men and help you hunt the bastards down.'

'Thanks,' J.P. said before I could reply. 'But Lute and me, we already decided that we're going to keep dogging the Guthries, day and night, till we got 'em dead to rights.'

Offended, Wyatt glared at me. 'Letting others do your talking for you now, Lute?'

'J.P.'s my partner,' I said. 'And he's right. We made a plan and we're sticking to it, no matter what.'

'Suit yourselves,' Wyatt said, steamed. 'But I warn you. When things go wrong, and they will, believe me, don't come to me begging for help, 'cause I won't lift a goddamn finger!' He stormed off.

J.P. and I exchanged grins.

'Tell the truth now,' J.P. deadpanned. 'Is there a sweeter-natured, more charming, lovable man than Mr. Wyatt Earp?'

'If there is,' I said, 'I'm sure the Good Lord snatched him up long ago.'

Chuckling, we headed for our horses.

# 21

I wasn't happy about swapping a comfortable bed for a blanket on the ground, but I guessed J.P. had his reasons for refusing Wyatt's offer so didn't say anything until we'd saddled up and had ridden a mile or so out of town. Then as we continued following the Guthries' tracks by moonlight, I couldn't contain myself any longer and reining up, said: 'Look, J.P., it's none of my business, but I've got to ask. What's the problem between you and Wyatt?'

'Difference of opinion.'

''Bout what?'

'Being a lawman.'

I sensed he had more to say so kept silent.

'I was in Tombstone last March right after Morgan was murdered,' J.P. continued after a pause. 'I'd witnessed a stagecoach robbery in January and

212

was summoned to court to give evidence. Afterward, out of respect, I went to Morgan's funeral. The next day while I was having lunch with his brother, Warren, Wyatt came into the saloon and got into a big brouhaha with one of the customers. It was over a silver-mine the man owned and Wyatt wanted a piece of it. It got real ugly and Warren, not wanting mirrors and furniture broken if it came to blows, told Wyatt and the man to take their quarrel outside. The man didn't want to go — it was obvious he was afraid of Wyatt — but Wyatt dragged him out and a little later, as I was leaving, I saw them arguing in the alley. I only stopped for a moment, but I heard Wyatt threaten to arrest the man for attempted robbery if he didn't make him a half-share partner. When the man called him on it, saying the charges were false, Wyatt said he didn't care: he'd find witnesses to swear on his behalf so that the judge believed him.' J.P. sighed, troubled by the memory and then said: 'That wasn't the first time I'd heard Wyatt abusing his authority as a lawman to browbeat someone over trumped-up charges. But since on both occasions I'd figured it wasn't any of my business, I didn't interfere — which doesn't say much for my integrity, I know, but I didn't feel good about stepping on another lawman's toes.' J.P. sighed again, before adding: 'I don't know how the first incident turned out, but this last time, after I'd finished my testimony and left the courthouse, I bumped into Warren and he told me that the man had signed over the mine to Wyatt and then left town.'

'Who was this fella, do you remember?'

'His name was Stokes — Gerald C. Stokes. Do you know him?'

'Uh-uh.'

'Ever heard of him?'

'Uh-uh. Probably some fly-by-night easterner trying to get rich overnight.'

'Not anymore,' J.P. said darkly. 'They

found his body — or what was left of it after the coyotes got through with it — beside the trail a few miles out of town. Had a .30–30 slug in the back of his head.'

'Jesus! Did they ever find out who bushwhacked him?'

'Nope. Probably never will, either. Not with Wyatt holding the reins.'

'Whoa! You saying Wyatt shot him?'

'No. I ain't saying that at all. Oh, sure, Wyatt's certainly capable of killing anyone he thinks is in his way or out to get him, but he's no bushwhacker and he sure as hell is no coward. And in my book, only a coward bushwhacks someone — 'specially from behind.'

I couldn't argue with that.

'Funny thing is,' J.P. went on, 'the mine never paid off for Wyatt. The S.O.B. only owned it for a few weeks and then lost it in a poker game.'

'Easy come, easy go,' I said. 'Story of Mr. Earp's life.'

'Amen,' J.P. said. 'Trouble is, ever since the O.K. Corral, and the fame that came with it, Wyatt's started to believe in his own legend. And when a lawman does that, he thinks he's above the law. And then everyone, good or bad, is in trouble. And that's where we stand right now. And as long as Wyatt Earp is riding point, that's where we'll always stand.' J.P. paused and grinned. 'End of sermon.'

Normally I would have laughed. But I knew J.P. was right and I hated to accept the fact. Naïve as it sounds, especially coming from a roustabut like me, I want to believe there's enough good in folks for it to one day rise to the top — even if I don't live long enough to see it.

J.P., misunderstanding my prolonged silence, said: 'Go ahead. Ask me.'

'Ask you what?'

'What's losing a mine and the previous owner getting killed got to do with my vendetta with Wyatt?'

'Okay. I'll bite. What's the connection?'

'There isn't one. 'Least, not one like

you think. My problem with Wyatt stems from another issue.'

'Go on.'

'Well, turns out he saw me watching him that day when he was threatening Stokes in the alley. Must've figured I heard him and when a few days after that Stokes gets bushwhacked, Wyatt now believes I think he's responsible and is spreading rumors about him. And though no one ever accused him of it, he blames me for everyone in Tombstone wondering if he pulled the trigger.'

'Go on.'

'Well, because I'm the only witness to what went on in the alley and, as such, can supply a motive for why he might want to kill Stokes, he decides he's got to get rid me. So from that day on, he's done everything he could to prod me into a showdown.'

'Sounds like Wyatt,' I said, adding: 'If it ever does come to that, take your time when you draw and make the first shot count. Wyatt isn't fast but he's damned accurate.'

'Thanks, I'll remember that,' J.P. said. 'But I don't see a shootout ever happening. I don't rile easy and outside of Wyatt calling me yellow, which I doubt even he'll do, I've no intention of slapping leather with him or any other lawman.'

We rode until the moon was almost directly overhead, its brilliant silvery light making it easy for J.P. to follow the Guthries' tracks, and only when our horses were ready to drop did we stop and make camp in a sheltered gully. As we were spreading our bedrolls a wind sprang up and tumbleweeds went bouncing past us. They made the horses jittery. Afraid that they may suddenly bolt, we hobbled them by a patch of nearby grass.

Though it was numbingly cold J.P. and I were too tired to bother building a fire and we climbed into our bedrolls as soon as we'd relieved ourselves. I can't sleep if I'm cold, especially since I've gotten older, so I pulled the blanket over my head and waited for my shivering to stop. It took me a while to warm up, but once I did I closed my eyes and was dozing off when a distant coyote yip-yipped at the moon. I don't know if the mournful howling waked J.P., but almost at once he whispered: 'You awake, Lute?'

I was tempted to ignore him. But deciding he might have something important on his mind I acknowledged him with a grunt.

'I been thinking . . . '

Another grunt.

'The Guthrie brothers . . . '

'What about 'em?'

'Been trying to pin down who they're selling guns to . . . '

'Mescaleros or Chiricahuas most likely.'

'Yeah, that's what I figured, too.'

'But?'

'Well, this is just a guess, but because we're so close to the Dragoons, it's possible the Guthries are dealing with one of the different bands that make up the Chiricahuas, like, say, the Nednai or Bedonkohes — '

That got my attention. 'Geronimo, you mean?'

'I don't know. I'm just saying it's possible.'

'Wonderful,' I said. 'Got any more pleasant bedtime thoughts?'

J.P. chuckled ruefully. 'So what do you think?'

The idea of going up against Geronimo brought back my shivers. 'It ain't too late to turn around, you know.'

'The same thought crossed my mind.'

'And?'

J.P. shrugged. 'Half of me says turn around, the other half says keep going.'

I thought long and hard before saying: 'Be a shame to quit now after all we've gone through.'

'Reading my mind again.'

'Then let's keep going.'

'Fair enough,' J.P. said. 'Till death do us part.'

'Sweet dreams to you too, *hombre*.'

J.P. didn't answer and I figured he'd fallen asleep. I closed my eyes and felt myself dozing off. It was then that Geronimo's scowling fierce-eyed face appeared before me. I must have been holding a gun in my dream because I put a bullet in his forehead. Blood spurted everywhere. Geronimo's face laughed mockingly at me. I shot him again and again. Finally Geronimo's bloody, bullet-riddled face disappeared. So did my shivering. I felt myself drifting off again, falling deeper and deeper into the silent, empty darkness. I heard myself asking where I was. No one answered. I wasn't surprised. Because, as we all know, that's a question no one can answer.

The last thing I remembered was thinking how ironic it would be if we really did come up against Geronimo since he and his little band of renegades had successfully managed to elude half the cavalry of the United States Army!

# 22

Sunup came too soon. Every part of my body ached and when I swallowed, my saliva tasted like tar. I grudgingly cracked open my eyes and saw that J.P. was already up and dressed. He was sitting on a nearby rock, a mug of water perched atop his knees, shaving himself in a shard of broken mirror.

'We might need that water later,' I warned him.

J.P. stopped shaving, wiped the soap from the blade of his Bowie and grinned at me. 'No sweat. Plenty more where that came from.' To prove his point, he picked up his canteen and held it upside down so that water poured from it.

'You've either gone *loco*,' I said, 'or you've found a creek.'

'More like a natural waterhole. Behind those rocks.' He thumbed at some nearby rocks that were smooth and milky white in color. 'Almost fell into the damn thing while I was stumbling around in the dark looking to take a piss.'

'Ah, the rewards of urination,' I said, adding: 'Behind those rocks, did you say?'

'Yeah. Why the look?'

'What look?'

'As if I'd just stepped into quick-sand.'

I hesitated, milking my pause, then said: 'I was wondering.'

''Bout what?'

'The water — you ain't drunk any of it yet, have you?'

'W-Why?' J.P. said, frowning. 'What's wrong with it?'

'Hopefully, nothing.'

'What makes you say that?'

I shrugged but didn't say anything.

'Listen,' J.P. said, 'I'm telling you, Lute, that water's fine.'

'If you say so.'

'I *do* say so,' J.P. insisted.

'Then you got nothing to worry about.' I sat up, pulled on my jeans and boots, stood up and crossed to the milky white rocks. Leaning over them, I saw a small natural hole in the ground on the other side. It was filled with brackish water. I sighed, loud enough for J.P. to hear.

'Now what's wrong?' he asked.

'It's like I figured,' I said soberly.

'Meaning?'

'Meaning you can thank your lucky stars you didn't drink any of this.'

J.P. didn't say anything but his expression told me he already had. 'Why? What's wrong with it?' he asked when he finally found his voice.

'P.A.P.'

'W-What's P.A.P.?'

'Phosphatase alkali poisoning,' I said, my tone hinting that he must be illiterate not to know this. 'Hell, the water's saturated with it.'

J.P. gulped. 'H-How do you know?'

'Well, first off by the taste, of course, and secondly, by the color. But even without drinking it or looking at it, you can tell by how white these rocks are.' I thumbed at the rocks. 'It's a dead giveaway, *amigo*.'

'It is?'

'Sure. I'll tell you, J.P., you may not realize it but you just dodged a bullet. If you'd swallowed any of this water, twenty minutes from now you'd be doubled over in agony with belly pains, and then, when they got so bad you'd be rolling around on the ground screaming — you'd start to go blind and froth would dribble out of the mouth and shortly after that, hell, you'd be dead. What's more, you'd be damned glad you were. But of course,' I said with a cheerful smile, 'since you didn't drink any water, you don't have a thing to worry about.' Before he could say anything, I moved off, whistling, and took a leak behind some other rocks.

When I'd finished and shaken the dew off my lily, I returned to camp and started folding my bedroll.

J.P., who had his back to me, was slowly rubbing his belly.

Somehow managing not laugh, I said: 'Do you reckon we got time for coffee or do you want to start after these yahoos right away?'

For a long moment J.P. didn't answer. Then he turned to me, his normally ruddy cheerful face a sickly pasty white, and said: 'I lied, Hoss.'

'Lied? 'Bout what?'

'The water. I did drink some. Right 'fore I started shaving.'

'Oh, shit,' I exclaimed, ' — you *didn't*?'

J.P. nodded glumly. 'How was I supposed to know? Hell, I grew up in the southwest and I've never even heard of this P.A.P. whatever you call it.'

'That's incredible,' I said. 'I mean everyone I know has heard of it or knew *someone* who had it.' I paused to let him sweat a little before adding: ''Course, there is one hope.'

'What's that?'

'It's possible that you could be one of

those rare cases.'

'Rare cases?'

'Someone who's immune to the poison.'

J.P. brightened immediately. 'You really think so? I mean, I may not die from it?'

I nodded but made sure I looked doubtful. 'Anything's possible, J.P. But I wouldn't get my hopes up, if I was you. Not until your twenty minutes is up anyway.'

'N-No, no, I'm not, but . . . I mean, how will I know if I am immune?'

'That's simple,' I said, picking up my saddle and blanket. 'You won't die.'

'What about the pains you mentioned — will I still get them?'

'I don't know. Maybe . . . ' I shrugged. 'I'm no doctor, J.P.'

'No, no, I know, but you are familiar this phos-pa-tas — alkali poisoning, right?'

'I've heard 'bout it, yeah.'

'So, what's your guess?'

I shrugged. 'Well, if you're pushing

me for an answer, then I reckon the only way you'll know for sure is if in an hour or so, you ain't rolling 'round in agony.' Going to my horse, I turned my back on J.P. so he wouldn't see me stifling my laughter and saddled up.

Behind me, I heard J.P. muttering agitatedly and wondered if I'd over-played the joke and should tell him the truth. But then I remembered how he'd pretended he was a drunk and never mentioned it to me, a fellow lawman, and decided there was no way in hell that I was going to let him off the hook. 'Least, not for a while anyway . . .

# 23

Though last night's moonlight was brighter than this morning's pale dawn light, J.P.'s keen eyesight had no problem picking up the hoof prints of the Guthrie brothers' horses. In fact he'd gotten so used to looking at them that he didn't even need to pick out the cracked hoof print, which made his task even easier.

As we rode through the many steep-sided ravines, arroyos, colorful red-rock canyons and across stretches of open desert as flat as any lake J.P. followed the tracks with such ease we never even slowed down. Though I was grateful, it made me realize just how poor my eyesight had gotten and I was forced to admit to myself that sooner rather than later I was going to have to wear spectacles. It wasn't a cheerful thought and for the first time in my life

I seriously considered giving up being a lawman.

After about an hour of riding, J.P. reined up and turned to me, a look of relief on his youthful sunburned face.

'Reckon I don't got it, Lute,' he said eagerly. 'Wouldn't you say?'

I hesitated, on the verge of prolonging his torture, but then decided he'd suffered enough mental anguish. 'Yeah, I'd say. Reckon you really are one of those rare cases all right. You sure are lucky, *hombre*. I've only known one other fella who was immune — ' I broke off as I saw puffs of smoke rising from a clifftop about a mile a north of us, then added: 'Looks like we've reached the end of the rainbow.'

J.P. stared uneasily at the rising smoke signals. 'Apaches?'

'That'd be my guess.'

'Can you read what it says, Hoss?'

I studied the smoke for a few moments before saying: 'It's not Apaches. It's the Guthries. They're telling whoever is buying the rifles where to meet them.'

'Where?' demanded J.P.

'*Barrancas del Cobre.*'

'Never heard of it. You?'

'Sure. Copper Canyon's one of a bunch of connecting canyons 'bout two miles west of here — as the crow flies.'

'You ever been there, Hoss?'

'Yeah, but only as far as the outer canyons. I never rode from one end to the other. And I'd wager, neither did any other white man looking to keep his hair. It's a rat's nest of renegade Apaches, most of them so hostile that not even Cochise, when he was alive, could control them.'

Ahead, the trail split into two distinct forks. I took the lead and followed the left fork as it wound its way deeper and deeper into canyon country. We followed the Guthries' tracks through one sheer-sided canyon after another, each one seemingly more remote and threatening than the last. I say threatening because we were now deep in Apache territory. I wasn't unfamiliar with the area, but no one knows the land like the

Indians who live there; especially if those Indians are Apache. They become as one with it — just like any rock, tree or creek — in a way that's impossible for a white man. An old Indian scout I knew once described the difference between a white man and an Apache's relationship to the land by simply saying: 'We got blood in our veins, they got dirt.'

We rode on, neither of us saying a word. It was as if we were reluctant to break the silence, like one is reluctant to break the silence in church, knowing at the same time that if we did speak, we'd speak in hushed respectful tones so as not to disturb the reverence that existed in the House of God.

Well, we were in Nature's church now and that same reverence seemed to exist around us. It was a truly unique feeling. We were absolutely alone. There wasn't a sign of life. Not an ant. Not a lizard. Not a sidewinder. Not even a high-flying hawk. Nothing!

Equally eerie, there was no wind or

breeze to moan faintly in our ears. All around us it was dead calm. It was the strangest damn thing. I know what I'm going to say doesn't make sense, but it's true nonetheless. I know because I've experienced it. On rare occasions there is a silence that is so complete, so absolutely quiet that it becomes a sound all of its own, a sound that can be deafening. This silence could have been that kind of silence if it hadn't been for our horses. The sound of their hooves click-clacking over the stony ground shattered the silence and caused echoes to bounce off the cliffs.

I'm not a man who runs scared. Nor do I get nervous easily. But I have to admit that the deeper we got into canyon country, the more tense and uneasy I felt. I think J.P. felt the same way, because I could hear him nervously humming *Dixie* to himself, as if to bolster his morale.

Finally, we reached the entrance to the fourth canyon. 'Okay,' I said, reining up. 'This is as far as I've ever gone, so from here on in your guess is as good as mine.' Grabbing my Winchester, I levered in a round and rested the rifle across my saddle horn, one finger around the trigger.

Beside me J.P. did the same. He licked his lips and looked around uneasily before saying: ''Fore we ride any farther, Hoss, there's something I'd like to know.'

'Shoot.'

'I ain't had much dealings with Indians and what dealings I've had was with Kiowas and Comanches. They can be blood-thirsty, like all Indians, but if you treated them fairly and like men, not ignorant savages, mostly they could be reasoned with.'

'So what's your question?'

'If it does turn out that the Guthries are dealing with Geronimo, do you reckon we can reason with him . . . make him understand that he ain't the one we're after?'

'Not a chance in hell,' I said. 'I've never dealt with him myself, but I've known plenty of fellas that have and to a man, they claim he's mean to the bone. Blames all whites for what the Mexicans did to him when he was young.'

'Killed his mother, wife and three children, you mean?'

'Yeah, while he was out hunting. From that day on, from all reports, he lives on hate and revenge.'

J.P. didn't say anything.

We kicked our horses up and rode into the canyon. I glanced at J.P. out the corner of my eye. He looked straight ahead, his tight-lipped expression similar to a man going to his own execution.

We rode through two more canyons, both similar to one another, and still saw no sign of any kind of life. But that all changed as we entered the next canyon. Though smaller than the previous canyons its tall reddish-orange cliffs were riddled with caves. The outer rock around the mouth of each cave was blackened by smoke, indicating that they had been or were still inhabited. There was also a network of man-made paths connecting the caves, further proof that we weren't alone. I didn't see anyone watching us, but just to be safe I kept swiveling my eyes so I'd be able to see anyone making a threatening move.

J.P. started to say something about the caves, but I cut him off. 'I see them,' I said quietly.

'What do you think we should we do?'

'Nothing. Just keep on riding and act like they aren't there.'

J.P. obeyed me and we rode on past cave after cave, some at ground level, others halfway up the cliff-face, without any mishap. It was damned unnerving and I almost wished the red devils would make their move, so at least we'd know where we stood.

J.P. must have felt the same way because as we neared the end of the canyon, he whispered: 'What do you figure they're up to, Lute? You think they're waiting for us to pass so they can then close in behind us and cut off our escape?'

'That would make sense. I'll tell you this though,' I said, 'whatever their plan is I wish to hell they'd get on with it so we'd known what we're up against.'

J.P. started to reply then stopped as we heard rifle shots coming from the canyon ahead of us. We both reined up and listened intently. At first it sounded like a gunfight. But as the shooting increased, each wild burst of gunfire was followed by frenzied whooping and yelling and I realized what was happening.

'Apaches,' I said. 'Bastards are celebrating. They must have just gotten the rifles from the Guthrie brothers.'

'In other words, we're too late?' J.P. said glumly.

'Never say die,' I said with a cheerfulness I didn't feel. ''Least now we know where the Guthries are.'

'And Geronimo,' J.P. reminded. ' — if it's him they're dealing with.'

'There's one sure way to find out.' I dug my spurs into the mare. She responded by giving an angry little buck and then charged ahead. I didn't look back but heard J.P. hollering at me to wait. I reined in a little, and within a few moments he caught up.

'It'd serve you right,' he grumbled, 'if I let you fight the Guthries and Geronimo alone.'

'Maybe that's my plan,' I replied.

'What do you mean?'

'Maybe I'm in on this rifle selling? Ever think of that?'

His expression said he hadn't.

'Think about it. It would explain why no one shot at us back at the caves.'

J.P. suddenly looked worried; then, not wanting to believe me, gave a nervous laugh.

'If that's true, Hoss, why'd you bring me along? Hell, you could've gotten rid of me plenty of times 'fore now.'

'And have you spill the beans 'bout the Guthries selling guns to the Apaches and rob me of my share of the take? Not a chance. Sides, I wasn't sure of the exact location where the trade was going to take place. I needed your eyes to track the Guthries down for me.'

Now J.P. looked even more worried.

I couldn't take it any longer. 'Oh, for chrissake,' I exclaimed. 'If you ain't the most gullible sonofabitch I ever did meet. I swear I could make up anything and you'd believe me.'

J.P. looked relieved and then indignant. 'Ha! You didn't fool me. Hell, I knew all along you was funning with me.'

'You did?'

''Course. I wasn't born this morning, you know.'

'Is that so? Then I guess you also knew all along that there's no such thing as P.A.P?'

J.P. reined up and frowned at me. 'No such — ? Mean you made it all up?'

'From start to finish.'

'Why the hell did you do that?'

'For the same reason you 'conveniently' forgot to tell me that you were only playing drunk when we met.'

'That was different. I didn't know you then. Didn't know if I could trust you or — '

'I'm a lawman. Same as you. That's all the trust you needed.'

'There's crooked lawmen. Said so yourself.'

I didn't remember saying any such thing. But he was right about crooked lawmen, so I shrugged and said: 'Fine. Chalk one up for you. Now, what's it going to be? Are we even and we let it go at that or do you want to continue?'

'No, no. We're even.'

'Fair enough. Then let's you and me go do what we came for: to get those goddamn rifles!' I spurred the mare, and after her customary rebellious buck, she broke into a steady loping gallop.

But this time I wasn't alone. J.P., now used to my sudden departures, had kicked up his horse at the same time and was riding alongside me.

That was something I really liked about J.P. He was a fast learner!

# 24

The Apaches and Guthrie brothers were in the last canyon. We heard the braves whooping before we saw them. When we got close to the entrance leading into the canyon I reined up, turned to J.P. and pointed to a steep narrow path that wound up the cliff-face. At the top of the path, there was a narrow opening that was too small to be a cave but perfect as a lookout site. It was halfway up the cliff-face, and from it anyone could see what was going on in the adjoining canyon. I mimed to J.P. that we should climb up to the opening. He nodded to show he understood, grabbed his rifle and field glasses and dismounted.

I did the same. We then tied up our horses behind some rocks and scrambled up the path. It was no easy climb, especially in the intense heat, and we were dripping with sweat by the time we reached the opening. It was about six feet across and four feet deep. We got on our bellies and slid our legs and the lower half of our bodies backward into the narrow opening. Then propped up on our elbows, we focused our glasses on the Guthrie brothers and the dozen or more excited braves.

The Guthries stood beside three crates that had been broken open. New .450 Martini-Henry carbines were stacked inside two of the crates. I could see their barrels glinting in the sunlight. The third crate held boxes of ammunition. Bryce and Gibby were handing the carbines to the Apaches, while Dokes — his wounded arm in a makeshift sling — gave each warrior a handful of cartridges.

The joyful Apaches started dancing and brandishing their carbines, quickly working themselves into a wild frenzy.

Refocusing, I slowly moved my glasses over the faces of each brave, looking for Geronimo. He wasn't among them. Disappointed, I was about to say something to J.P. when he nudged me and pointed to a rock a short distance from the Guthrie brothers.

I focused on the rock and there sat Geronimo, clutching an old Springfield 1873 trapdoor rifle, watching the proceedings. Magnified by the lenses, his lined, swarthy, scowling face looked older and even crueler than it did in the photos I'd seen of him. I moved in on his dark smoldering eyes. Shaded by his protruding brow, they were filled with an intense seething hatred that was frightening even from a distance.

Beside me, J.P. tapped my arm. Lowering my glasses, I turned to him.

'What you mentioned earlier,' he said, ''bout it not being too late to turn around — I'm thinking now that ain't such a bad idea.'

Even though he was joking, I detected a hint of fear in his voice — the same fear that I'd felt moments earlier.

'Just say the word,' I said, playing along, 'and I'll be right behind you.'

'What about the Guthries?'

'We can always hunt them down later.'

'You're reading my mind again, Hoss.'

'That still leaves Geronimo — what do we do about him?'

'Let the army handle the sonofabitch.'

'Now you're talking,' I said. 'The undertakers will love that idea.'

'Undertakers?'

'Sure. They'll get rich making coffins for all the troopers that are going to die on account of those new carbines.'

J.P. lost his grin and all the laughter disappeared from his clear blue eyes.

'You sure know how to shoot a fella's horse out from under him,' he said, adding: 'You do understand I was funning with you, right?'

'If I didn't, *amigo*, I would've shot you for real long ago.'

Relieved, J.P. said: 'Well, the good news is we got surprise on our side.'

'I was thinking the same thing, *hombre.*' I looked down at the Apaches dancing wildly around the Guthrie brothers and thought what I wouldn't give for a Gatling gun or a few sticks of dynamite.

'So how do you want to play this?' J.P. asked.

'Reckon we only got two choices. Stay up here and pick off as many as we can, which most likely wouldn't be too many — '

'Or?'

'Climb down and try to get close enough so we can force them to throw down their guns.'

J.P. chewed his lip and looked dubious. 'If they was all white men, Hoss, I'd go along with you. But we're dealing with a bunch of goddamn savages here. I mean, who the hell knows *how* they'll react?'

I started to agree with him and then stopped as below us the Guthrie brothers, who'd been examining the gold dust that Geronimo had given them in two small sacks, suddenly drew their guns and opened fire on the unsuspecting braves.

Several were killed instantly, while the others stumbled around in confusion.

Not Geronimo. He'd been watching the brothers. And as they drew their Colts, he leaped down from the rock and took cover behind it. His cat-quick reflexes saved his life. Doke was already shooting at him, the bullets ricocheting off the rock near the aging chief's head.

The braves, now recovered from the surprise attack, angrily loaded their carbines, aimed at the Guthrie brothers and pulled the triggers.

I figured the Guthries were done for. But nothing happened.

Laughing, the three brothers continued firing at the Apaches, killing more of them.

'*Sonofabitch!*' I said. 'Those bastards filed off the firing pins!'

J.P. acted before I'd finished speaking. Taking quick aim, he fired at Gibby.

His bullet hit the middle brother in the thigh. Gibby went down, clutching his leg and writhing in pain.

I put my sight on Doke and shot him in the chest, sending him sprawling.

Bryce, seeing his brothers get shot, panicked and sprinted for the nearest rocks.

He never made it. Geronimo pulled a small ax from his belt and hurled it at Bryce.

The youngest Guthrie screamed as the ax buried in his back and pitched onto his face. He desperately tried to get up and when he couldn't, began crawling toward the rocks.

But the braves quickly closed in around him, blocking his escape.

They pulled him up and dragged him, struggling and cursing, to Geronimo.

'You mightn't want to watch this,' I told J.P. 'It ain't going to be pretty.'

'I've seen folks scalped before,' he said.

'Suit yourself.'

Geronimo said something to his

warriors and they dragged Bryce over to a dead, leafless oak that defied all odds by growing out from between two rocks. Using rawhide, the braves tied Bryce to the tree and began shooting arrows into him from close range.

I was right. It wasn't pretty. The Apaches made sure none of their arrows hit a vital organ and Bryce soon looked like a human pincushion.

He screamed and writhed as each arrow sank into him. Blood streamed from his wounds until his whole body was a glistening red.

'Jesus Mary'n Joseph,' J.P. breathed. 'I know he killed your brother, Hoss, but how long we going to let 'em keep this up?'

I looked at him. 'You shoot him now,' I warned, 'and we'll end up taking his place.'

Sobered by my words, J.P. rolled over onto his back, facing me so that he didn't have to watch Bryce suffering. But he couldn't shut out Bryce's screams. And he couldn't stop reacting to the pain that he knew Bryce must be feeling.

Eventually even I'd had enough.

Rising, I picked my way down the steep rocky slope to the bottom. Loose stones and dirt came slithering down around me, the noise attracting Geronimo's attention.

He yelled something to his braves and as one, they stopping shooting arrows at Bryce and faced me.

There aren't words to describe how scared I felt. But remembering comments from the men who'd had dealings with Geronimo, I knew that the only hope I had of surviving was to show the old chief that I wasn't afraid of him.

Holding my rifle down at my side, I marched straight toward Geronimo, trying as I did not to show any fear.

The braves grew restless and one of them started to draw an arrow back in his bow.

Geronimo barked at him and the shamed warrior lowered his weapon.

I stopped when I was within three paces of Geronimo and greeted him in Spanish. I'm not fluent in Spanish but I figured he might consider it a sign of respect if I at least tried to talk to him in a language he not only understood but used frequently.

For a moment that seemed to last for hours he didn't reply. His glowering, cruel-eyed expression didn't change either. Inwardly my courage sank. But outwardly I somehow managed to hide my fears.

Finally, Geronimo spoke. He answered me in Spanish, his voice gruff and harsh and though I didn't understand everything he said, I grasped enough to know that in his own way he was greeting me and at the same time, demanding to know what I wanted.

I pointed at the blood-soaked body of Bryce and then at my Winchester.

The braves immediately grew angry and shook their weapons at me.

Geronimo snapped at them and they fell silent.

'This White Eyes,' he said to me in English, 'he is friend?'

'No. Enemy.'

Geronimo's eyebrows arched in surprise.

'You wish to kill?'

I nodded.

He studied me with his fierce dark eyes, said: '*Bueno*.'

Taking this to mean that I could kill Bryce, I raised my rifle.

Immediately, Geronimo barked at me in Spanish and raised his hand threateningly.

'You kill like Apache,' he said in English. Before I could reply, he spoke to one of his warriors. Grudgingly, the brave drew his knife and threw it at my feet. It stuck, blade-first, in the dirt.

'Now you kill,' Geronimo told me. 'We watch.' He covered me with his rifle, the menacing look in his eyes warning me not to argue.

Pulling the knife from the ground, I walked toward Bryce. The braves sullenly parted, allowing me to pass.

I stopped in front of Bryce. There were at least a dozen arrows stuck in him. Pain had frozen his horrified expression. Though he was slowly bleeding to death he somehow managed to lift his head and look at me. His eyes were bloodshot and showed no sign of recognition, and I realized he didn't remember me.

His cracked and bloodied lips moved with great difficulty. It may have been wishful thinking, but I think I heard him beg me to kill him.

I thought of my brother, Heck, and of how much I'd lost because of this man and his brothers. I looked into Bryce's eyes. It was only for a moment but in that moment I tried to forgive him. I couldn't. Worse, God forgive me, I truly enjoyed his suffering.

Then I plunged the knife into his chest.

I thought I'd stabbed him without any emotion. But as the blade sank in up to the hilt and Bryce gasped, I realized how much anger I felt toward him and how satisfying it was to finally kill him.

He died almost immediately. I turned and faced Geronimo and the half-circle of angry braves who stood watching me.

'*Gracias, señor*,' I said to Geronimo. 'You have done me a great favor.'

'*Por nada*,' he said, shrugging. 'It is good to kill one's enemies.'

I nodded.

He held something out to me. I saw it was the two small sacks containing the gold dust. Printed on each sack was HOPE MINING CO. and I guessed that Geronimo had killed the miners who'd found the gold.

'You take,' Geronimo said.

I knew there was enough gold dust in those sacks to make my life comfortable. But something in Geronimo's eyes warned me that he was testing me and I shook my head.

'You not like gold, *señor*?' he said.

'Not when it is stolen,' I replied.

I'm not sure but I think I glimpsed

respect in Geronimo's eyes.

Hoping I was right, I said: 'Do I and my *amigo* have the great chief's permission to leave now?'

Geronimo didn't answer for so long I feared he was going to refuse.

Certainly by the look on the faces of his braves they were hoping he would.

'*Si*,' he said at last. '*Tu puedes ir.*' Then, as if it was an afterthought: '*Via con Dios.*'

'*Via con Dios*,' I said. Turning, I started back toward the foot of the slope where J.P. stood awaiting me.

I felt the sun burning on my back. But it didn't burn as much as the hatred I knew was coming from his braves as they glared after me.

As I approached J.P. the relief on his face was almost comical.

'Relax,' I told him. 'Smile.'

'Is the S.O.B. really letting us go?'

For a moment I was tempted to throw a scare into him by saying no. But I decided this was no time for humor; this was a time to get away from

Geronimo before he changed his mind and used us for target practice.

'Yep,' I said. 'He really is.'

J.P. expelled a sigh of relief that could have been heard all the way to Texas.

'Hoss,' he said as we walked to our horses, 'if I live to be a hundred I'll never be able to repay you for saving my life.'

'Don't be so sure,' I said, straight-faced. 'As my full-time deputy, you may learn to regret those words.'

J.P. looked at me, his expression a mix of delight and disbelief. 'You mean — ?'

I cut him off.

'Like you once said, *amigo*. Till death do us part . . . '

## TWO FROM TEXAS

### Neil Hunter

One of the men arrives in Gunner Creek at the end of a long search, whilst the other simply drifts into the town. Fate has drawn them together: two Texans who find a town in trouble — and, being who they were, have to throw in their hands to help. Chet Ballard and Jess McCall are Texicans down to the tips of their boots. Big men with hard fists and fast guns, who see trouble and refuse to back away from it . . .

# DERBY JOHN'S ALIBI

## Ethan Flagg

Derby John Daggert is out for revenge on his employer after a severe beating meted out for theft and adultery. Then a robbery goes badly wrong, two men are murdered, and the killer makes a wild ride from Querida to Denver. As prime suspect, Daggert is arrested, but his lawyer convinces the jury he was elsewhere when the crime was committed. It is left to Buckskin Joe Swann to hunt down the culprit — a task more difficult than he could have ever imagined . . .

# HOOD

## Jake Douglas

When he wakes wounded in the badlands, he doesn't even know his own name, where he is, or how he got there. He sure doesn't know who shot him and left him to die. But when the riders come to try and finish the job, they call him 'Hood' ... Under the scorching sun, he does the only thing he can: straps on a six-gun, gets back in the saddle, and sets out to find out who's on his trail ...

# THE RECKLESS GUN

## Dale Graham

A stagecoach rattles its way across the Mogollon Plateau, carrying a cargo of gold bullion. Passenger Lucy Calendar, the new schoolteacher at Casa Grande, is fearful of being attacked by Dutch Henry Vandyke and his gang, and must trust in the mounted bluecoats escorting the vehicle. But the soldiers are relieved by strangers at Sedona — and when the coach is held up further along the trail, Lucy finds that not only has the Vandyke Gang infiltrated the escort, but Dutch Henry himself has been riding in the coach all along . . .

# BLIND-SIDED

## Billy Hall

When Ike Murdo fetches up in Chickasaw, looking for work, he's taken on at the U-V-Cross — only to find himself falling in love with its owner, the widowed Minerva Vogel. The affection proves mutual, and her two young children also warm to Ike. Everything seems to be going well. But Kameron Kruger of the neighbouring Bar-Bar-K is using more than his legal share of Hatfield Creek, depleting the U-V-Cross's water supply, and threatening to start a range war . . .

# MY NAME IS IRON EYES

## Rory Black

Riding his palomino stallion, Iron Eyes escorts Squirrel Sally's stage-coach through the town of Lobo. The infamous bounty hunter is weary, and the remote settlement seems a peaceful place to rest — but Iron Eyes is mistaken. As he steers his mount down the main street, his eyes light upon a row of tethered horses. His instincts flare when he realises that the black roan with the white-tipped tail belongs to Buffalo Jim McCoy, a fearsome outlaw worth five thousand dollars — dead or alive . . .